Avala

Annabel Barnett

For my Grandchildren:
Ben and Lorelei
Eliza and Marisa

Contents

Chapter 1

Only three more days to go, said Jack to himself. No more school, no more maths and no more Kicking Kieran and Nasty Nick. He allowed himself to feel just a little bit excited. But not too excited, said Jack to himself, knowing my luck something is bound to go wrong.

But the thought of the holidays kept tickling the edge of his brain and fluttering under his ribs. It was not just the end of term that he was looking forward to, but the knowledge that he was flying for the first time in his life. And if that was not exciting enough, he was not only flying out of dreary England, but going to the Alps for a *snowboarding* holiday!

It seemed both unreal and thrilling. Jack could not contain his happiness any longer, and he flung himself round the corner of the corridor with wild abandon. Who should he cannon into but Nasty Nick, who was walking backwards as he talked to Kicking Kieran and his mates behind him.

'Come here you little…' snarled Nick. But although Jack was small for his age, he was quick. He dodged past the group and ran outside. The bell was about to go signalling, the end of break, so he did not expect Nick and his friends to follow. But to his horror he realised they were right behind him! Frantically he ran round the building, but he could see his way was blocked by a group of older boys chatting to each other and strolling towards him, so he was forced to dodge into a yard that was out of bounds. It had a high wall. There were a few buildings that backed onto the wall. All of them had locked doors.

'I'm going to be trapped!' he squeaked.

That second, he noticed a tall plank propped up against the wall. Nimble as a squirrel, he ran up the sloping plank and climbed onto the wall. Nick came across the yard and made as if to follow him. Jack heaved at the long heavy plank to dislodge it. Nick pushed back, and then, without warning he pulled sharply instead. The sudden change of direction nearly dragged Jack off the top. He flung his arms out and fell spread-eagled on the top of the wall, dislodging old cement and lichen, and banging his chin hard.

'Now what are you going to do?' sneered Nick, as the plank clattered to the concrete. Jack realised that Nick had removed the only safe way back to the ground. To add to his misery, he felt his mobile slip out of his pocket and was too late to stop it clattering to the concrete and landing right by Nick's feet.

'Confiscated!' announced Nick triumphantly, putting Jack's mobile into the pocket.

At that moment the bell went for the beginning of lessons. The group of bullies circled under Jack for a few seconds, chucking small stones at him. Then they bolted for their classroom.

Jack looked down. It was a long way to jump. There was concrete on both sides. *I should never have imagined myself going on holiday*, he thought miserably.

If he jumped, he was certain to hurt himself. Then he would not be able to snowboard. He looked at the place where the roof of a shed joined the wall. Beyond the roof he could see a field.

Grass would be softer than concrete, he thought.

But first he would have to climb across the roof. He edged cautiously along the wall towards the roof. The roof was made of rusty corrugated iron. Very cautiously Jack climbed onto it. He could see where the bolts had been attached to the beams, but they had long since dropped out, leaving behind rusty holes. He crabbed his way along the roof. In the middle, the roof sagged under his weight. Jack stopped moving and held his breath. The silence was broken by a blackbird breaking cover and shrieking an alarm. It made Jack start. It took him a moment to gather his composure, then he shifted his weight. Gently he inched his way across the roof. He could hear his heart drumming in his ears. But despite sagging more, the roof held, and he managed to reach the wall. *Phew!* he thought. He could feel his legs trembling and for a moment he was forced to sit still while he worked out what to do next. The field looked much more inviting than the hard surface of the yard, but the wintry grass still looked a long way down.

Parked up close to the wall, Jack could see an old straw trailer. On each end of the trailer there were high iron guards that were designed to keep the straw bales in place. One of the iron guard rails was tantalisingly close to the top of the wall, but there was still a sizeable gap between the cross bar and the top. Jack edged his way along the wall so that he was opposite the straw trailer. Screwing up his courage he swung out from the wall and caught the bar. His legs followed swinging hard against a lower cross bar but, although it hurt, Jack held on tightly to the top rail and scrabbled madly with his feet until he found the next horizontal bar below him. He felt dizzy with relief when he found he could stand and catch his breath. Then he had to stretch his full length to climb down the guard and at last he could squirm onto the flat bed of the trailer. Although the trailer was high off the ground, it was a lot lower than the top of the wall and so he jumped. His feet stung but at least he was on terra firma. He raced back onto the school property before anyone should see him out of bounds and rushed into the classroom, flushed with success.

'Detention!' snapped Mrs Mottram his class teacher the moment she saw someone coming in late.

But she frowned when she realised that it was Jack. She was worried about him. He was usually a contented and uncomplicated lad who tried hard. But this term he had not been concentrating and seemed quite low on occasions.

'Come and see me afterwards Jack,' she ordered. But this time when she spoke, her voice was much softer.

'You're going to get off,' whispered Ben his best friend, nodding encouragingly.

At the end of the lesson the bell went and there was the usual burst of chatter. Jack quickly told Ben and a few others what had happened.

'You'd better watch out,' said one of his classmates. 'I know that Nick is going on a skiing holiday too. I bet he'll be at the same place as you!'

'What!' gasped Jack 'Oh no, he can't be.'
Overhearing, Mrs. Mottram looked at him and saw the horror in his face.

'Don't be ridiculous Jack,' she snapped 'I can think of at least six different European countries where you can ski, and all those countries have hundreds, if not thousands of ski resorts. The likelihood of you and Nick ending up in the same resort is millions to one. You'd be more likely to win the lottery,' she scoffed.

Jack felt slightly better.

'You'd better come and explain why you were late,' his teacher continued.

Jack wanted to tell Mrs. Mottram that Nasty Nick had taken his mobile, but only the Seniors were allowed mobiles. He looked at her and then looked down at the floor.

'You don't help yourself, you know Jack, going about with a long face. You have to stand up and look confident,' she sighed. 'Well it's been a long cold term and I for one don't want to spoil the holidays. I'll let you off this time.'

'Thanks Mrs. Mottram,' said Jack cheering up and he dashed out of the classroom with his teacher's, 'Don't run!' ringing in his ears.

The last few days of term came to an end and Jack began to dream of the holiday that lay before him.

He was going with his sister Sapphire. She was older than him and everybody called her Blue. His father was going too. Their parents had divorced a year ago and their father had been very despondent, but he now had a new special friend, or partner, as he called her. Her name was Marine and she was French. She was coming too. In fact, it was Marine who had organised the holiday; they were going to visit the Alpine town she had grown up in.

Neither Jack, nor Blue, knew Marine very well, but Blue was determined to dislike her.

Jack could see that Marine was pretty and she had a most delightful accent when she spoke English. But to tell the truth, Marine had *really* won Jack over when she had given him an inspired Christmas present! It was three lessons on a snowboard, in the Snow Dome.

Jack found most of his schoolwork difficult. His hand-eye co-ordination was poor, so he didn't feel good playing sport. In fact, he felt he was not much good at anything. But when it came to balancing, Jack discovered he had a wonderful skill.

The family had arrived at the Snow Dome. Blue and his father had chosen to take skis. Marine was watching from the side. The teacher who was a cheerful lad from New Zealand called Simon, gave Jack some instructions.

Jack edged off crouching over his board. He glided gently across the slope and then, by moving his weight on to the other edge of the snowboard, he came back again, passing his father who called out, 'Good man!'

Jack repeated the action and floated past Blue, 'Yay Jack!'

He glided past Marine watching on the side. 'Jack you are expert,' she called admiringly and, now much to the amazement of the instructor who had taken two quick turns to catch up, Jack was boarding past him too.

'Crikey, wait for the rest of us guys,' he joked.

But Jack would not, could not stop... the feeling of slipping down the slope was so thrilling. Not until he had travelled to the flat base of the hill did he stop. He sat down, hard on his bottom.

'Good on you!' applauded Simon. 'You're a natural!'

After three sessions in the Snow Dome Jack decided that snowboarding was the greatest sport in the world.

It was then that Marine organised the trip to her grandparents' hotel in a ski resort called Méribel. Even Blue had to admit that this was completely awesome. She had been on a week's skiing holiday with her school some two years earlier and was longing to go again.

Their Mum was brilliant at kitting them out with begged, borrowed and Oxfammed clothes. Jack thought that Blue would have liked new ski clothes, but to his surprise Blue had boasted to her friends that the ski clothes had come from Oxfam. Mum helped them pack.

'I wish you were coming Mum,' said Blue. 'We'll text every day.'

'I wish Ruff was coming,' said Jack as he put his arms round Ruff. Ruff slipped out of his arms to lie on his back. 'You have the softest tummy of any dog in the whole world,' Jack told him.

Seeing Ruff with all four legs in the air, Blue could not resist joining Jack scratching Ruff between his front legs, whilst laughing at Ruff's back leg bicycling in contented circles.

The day before they were due to travel, Marine took them all to visit her parents who lived in an old rectory in a little village about an hour away. Arriving they could see that the house was surrounded by a large garden, but unfortunately it was pouring with rain - too wet to investigate.

'What are we going to do?' muttered Blue crossly to Jack.

Marine's parents, Peter and Janine, greeted them politely but seemed anxious to talk to Marine and their father privately. At least very soon after they had arrived, Marine's mother suggested they run away and explore the house, including the 'grenier'.

'Attic,' translated Marine.

Blue and Jack were delighted to slip away from the adults and ran upstairs looking into every room. The house was large and cold. The bedrooms were sparsely furnished. Eventually they came to a spiral staircase that led clearly to the attic. This was a much more interesting place! At the top of the spiral staircase, there was a small landing and off it, there was a passage in the middle and four doors leading into rooms. Each room was full of all sorts of stuff. Old magazines piled high, a rocking horse that had lost its mane and some large awkward-looking dolls. There were big black trunks with names of the owners painted in white on the top. Blue became absorbed by beaded dresses hanging from one of the many clothes rails.

'Look at these Jack,' she called.

But Jack had moved to another room where he found all sorts of ancient skiing equipment. There were wooden skis with leather ties, some leather goggles and a huge wooden sledge. He caught sight of a massive fur-lined coat. One of the big pockets was gaping open in such an inviting way that Jack put his hand inside, where he felt something solid, and he pulled out a curious toy. It was a figure with furry feet and a leather overcoat. The face was furry too, the eyes were black and seemed particularly alive. It looked both human and bear like. Jack felt drawn towards the little figure. He put it deep into his own pocket.

From the depths of the house they could hear their father calling them.

'Coming!' they yelled in unison. It was fun half running down the stairs and half sliding down the banisters. Puffing slightly, they arrived into the study where the adults were waiting.

Turning to talk to Jack, Blue's eyes bulged, 'What's that in your pocket?' she gasped, then shrieked, 'Is it alive?'

Jack blushed as he realised that sticking out of the pocket was the top of the little figure.

'I found it upstairs in the attic,' he stammered as he took it out of his pocket to show Blue that it was not alive.

His father looked both embarrassed and cross, 'You shouldn't have it Jack,' he admonished.

'Oh! That little figure, it is always finding its way to unusual places,' laughed Marine's father. 'It's yours Jack!' he announced, clapping Jack on the back.

'I sink it belonged to my great grandfazzerrr,' added Marine's mother. 'It was a lucky, 'ow you say, charm? But when Peter brought me to England we had to bring all my grandfazzerr's belongings too and do you know Jack, sometimes I find it downstairs by the back door, and I cannot imagine 'ow it got there. I am sure it is a joke that this one is playing on me,' and she patted her husband on his arm.

'It's not me,' scoffed her husband, 'it's one of Maggie's kids.'

'But they always keep to the kitchen when Maggie is cleaning, or they are watching television and they are not allowed upstairs,' pointed out Marine's mother. 'The way this little creature moves around, I tell you Jack, it 'ees 'aunted,' but she added airily, 'though not in a bad way.'

'I think he should have asked first,' stated Jack's father, ignoring Marines mother's story.

'I am sure 'e was going to 'enry,' said Marine soothingly, making Jack warm to her even more.

'But please come on, we 'ave roast chicken for lunch,' urged Marine's mother and they followed her into the dining room. Jack stuffed the little figure into his pocket. But surprisingly it no longer seemed to fit. Its little topknot insisted on poking out in an incriminating way.

Quite soon after lunch, they said their goodbyes and thank yous. Jack blushing as he thanked Marine's parents for the odd little figure.
'Our pleasure old chap. It's been trying to escape this house for years!' Marine's dad winked at Jack and rolled his eyes in a disbelieving way towards his wife.

The rain had finally stopped. They had an easy ride back to their mother's house to have supper and do a final pack. Jack placed the figure on his bed and looked at it with disbelief. It was definitely bigger, it was now the size of a small bear he had had as a child.

'Blue!' he called, 'Come and look at this!'

'Oh, you've got two of them. Jack you didn't steal that one too?' gasped Blue.

'Don't be stupid, it's the same one!' said Jack urgently.

Blue looked at him and rolled her eyes, 'Dad will be really angry if he sees you stole two of them, better keep it here so he never sees,' she advised.

Jack took a breath in, to insist on his innocence, but at that moment Ruff came bounding in, then stopped. Quivering with excitement he fixed his eyes on the figure, he gave a little enquiring bark, and then he jumped up beside it. Keeping a small distance, he settled down next to it.

'You had better move it, or by the time we have had supper Ruff will have turned it into a thousand little pieces,' warned Blue, 'and then you will have only one.'

Somehow Jack knew that there was no point in arguing with Blue until he felt straight in his own mind about what he was seeing. He picked up the figure and put it on a high shelf. Ruff whined in a disappointed way, making Jack pleased he had moved the figure out of harm's way.

'Bedtime!' ordered his mother after supper, 'as you have to get up at an unearthly hour.'

Jack ran up to his room and there was the figure back on his bed, and Ruff sitting close by as if guarding it.

'Ruff … how did you?' began Jack looking up at the very tall shelf.

'You are the champion of champions in jumping,' he told his little dog shaking his head in amazement. He put the figure back on the shelf, this time stuffed behind some heavy books.

'Now try and get him,' he challenged Ruff.

Jack got ready for bed quickly and willed himself to sleep to make the morning come more quickly. This did not work it seemed ages before he went to sleep and only minutes before his mother was telling him it was time to get up as his father and Marine would be arriving soon to pick them up. At that moment there was a ring at the doorbell.

'Oh no, they're early' said his Mum 'Be as quick as you can!'

Jack did not need any encouragement and dragged on his clothes.

He went into the bathroom as he needed a pee, and to find his toothbrush and toothpaste. Only minutes later he heard his mother calling, so he grabbed his heavy backpack and went downstairs, meeting a yawning Blue on the way. Ruff ran beside him, all the time jumping up high as if to leap into his backpack.

'Sorry Ruff you can't come too,' Jack said to his little dog.

The hand over was a bit uncomfortable. Their mother had only met Marine once before, and because of the early hour everyone felt a bit subdued. Their Mum gave them a quick hug each.

'Have a lovely time' she called, shivering slightly for it was dark and cold outside.

They got into the warm car and waved and began their journey. About five minutes later their father asked if they had everything, and ignored Blue's comment of, 'A bit late now.'

Jack could not resist checking that he *did* have his passport and he undid the front pocket of his backpack, which seemed heavy and even more unwieldy than he remembered. He was reassured to see his passport, but amazed to see the furry figure stuffed in the back pocket right in front of him, and he was sure that it was a bit bigger.

'Did you put that in there?' he whispered accusingly to Blue.

'No, I did not,' replied Blue looking at him as if he was mad.

'Well, someone did and it wasn't me,' said Jack.

'Don't be ridiculous Jack!' scoffed Blue.

'Stop arguing,' ordered their father.

For the rest of the journey Jack tried to think how Ruff could have got up onto the shelf, then found his way behind the books and carefully placed the figure into Jack's backpack. It was all too fantastic and made him feel very uncomfortable.

They arrived in the airport terminal car park. There was a transit bus waiting.

'If we're really quick, we can catch that bus,' said Dad. And in the rush and excitement Jack totally forgot about the furry-faced figure for a moment.

As they approached the terminal they could see the planes taking off and landing. They grabbed a trolley and made their way through the huge revolving doors. The first thing that struck Jack was how massive the check-in area was. It was just as well that the hall was built like a warehouse because it was chock full of other people pushing trolleys, heaped with bags.

He put his backpack on the trolley, which now seemed unaccountably much lighter. On an impulse he checked the pocket with the passport. The figure was no longer there. Jack felt totally bewildered. He knew that no one else could have taken it out of the backpack pocket. He looked around wildly. Had the figure dropped out? He could see no sign of it.

They joined one of the many queues bound for Lyons.

'I just hope that's not a dead animal round her neck!' hissed Blue, when she saw Marine put on a cream ski jacket trimmed with fur.

Some more people arrived in the queue. It was impossible to tell who was in which line. Suddenly the queue which had seemed good natured, became restless, and two people each started to claim that the other was pushing in.

Why do they have to be like that, thought Jack to himself, chewing his bottom lip.

They heard shouts of surprise behind them and an indistinct shape was moving towards them. Suddenly over the shouts, everyone heard an awful cry that boomed around the building, bouncing amongst the steel struts in the ceiling. Nobody knew where to look, and someone screamed.

The shape came towards Jack and caught its foot on Marine's bag. For a moment, as the figure stumbled and nearly fell, its hood fell back and Jack looked at his furry figure's face, only now that face had a body that was as tall as his knees!

The figure's eyes met Jack's, and in that second Jack was mesmerised. It was if the terminal full of jostling people did not exist. Jack could hear himself say, 'Yes.' But he could not remember what the question was.

Jack was also aware that he could smell the bear-like figure. It was a nice smell. It reminded Jack of the countryside after rain. Jack had an impression of small furry feet, as the figure shifted slightly and vanished.

'What 'appened 'ere?' gasped Marine. Her bag had burst open, throwing her clothes and make up over the floor. Jack exchanged glances with Blue, who was looking both embarrassed and disapproving. Then Jack looked in the immediate area for the little figure. But apart from excited voices from people around him, there was no sign that it had ever been there! The airport security guards were looking round, clearly confused! Extra police had arrived but there was no sign of *the peculiar … the peculiar what?* wondered Jack.

The face of the hooded figure kept flashing across Jack's mind. He kept remembering its eyes, which had looked deep into his own eyes. *It was if he was trying to speak to me*, thought Jack, and dismissed the thought as ridiculous. But even at that moment, he could not get over the feeling that the figure was close by. In his mind Jack had a vision of the figure, it was gesturing him to open his backpack. As if in a dream Jack felt compelled to open the top of his backpack.

'No time for that Jack, we need to move forward,' said Henry, Jack's father.

'What are you looking for?' asked Blue.

'I don't know,' said Jack, feeling stupid. As Jack stared into his backpack, he felt something brush past his face.

'Get up Jack, we're moving,' ordered his father.

Eventually it was their turn to check in.

'Have you packed your bags yourselves?' asked the check-in woman brightly.

'Yes, with help from our Mum,' answered Blue loyally. The check-in woman smiled at her.

'Are you carrying anything given you by someone else?' she asked.

'No,' answered Blue.

She looked at Jack who felt strangely guilty when he too answered, 'No.'

'Put that bag on the scales to be weighed please,' said the check-in woman, pointing at Jack's bag. He heaved it on to the conveyor belt. For some reason it seemed much heavier than when he had brought it into the Departure Lounge.

'This one will have to be checked in, it is too big for hand luggage and it's overweight, so you'll have to pay the surcharge,' said the check-in woman to Jack's father.

'What do you mean, I've got to pay for it?' demanded his father, 'Whatever have you got in there, Jack?'

'Nothing,' replied Jack. 'It was alright when we weighed it at home,' he added defensively.

'I should have leant you one of mine. These old backpacks always weigh a ton,' replied his father not really listening. Jack watched his backpack travel along the conveyor belt, turn right and disappear. *I hope I see it again*, he thought.

Two hours later they were boarding the plane with all thoughts of the backpack forgotten. Blue let Jack sit by the window. There were various announcements and there was a moment when Jack thought they were moving, but it was another plane gliding past theirs. Then they really *were* moving. They travelled across the tarmac for what seemed like ages.

At the beginning of the runway Jack could hear the engines revving up. He could feel the power fighting the brakes. At last the Captain drove the plane down the runway and just as Jack thought they would never fly, the land dropped below him and there was a clunk as the wheels retracted.
'We're up!' he announced triumphantly to Blue.

'Let's see,' she said, leaning over him.

The two of them looked at the countryside dropping below them. The land looked extremely neat. There were regular patches of green and brown, neatly lined with hedges. White lines of frost sat on the north side of the fields. Jack identified a motorway stretched out under him. He had a sudden thought, *I wonder if any of those drivers can see this plane and are wondering where it is going?* He felt that bubbles of excitement were exploding behind his belly button.

'I just can't wait till we get there!' he grinned at Blue, who grinned back.

An hour and half later the plane flew over the edge of the Alps, and even though the plane was several thousand metres up, the mountains still looked magnificent. More importantly they were covered in snow.

Eventually the Captain announced they were landing. They lost height and the engine made a different sound. Then they circled around the airport that Jack could see below. The plane dropped sharply, and they flew just a few metres over the airport fence. The Captain landed the plane onto the runway where it bounced once. There was a terrific noise of the engines as they worked hard to bring the plane to a stop. *Wow, that was exciting,* said Jack to himself.

In the airport there was a certain amount of chaos whilst everyone claimed their luggage. Jack's dad had hired a car and they loaded it up. Soon they were driving through a valley with steep cliffs to one side and slopes leading gradually to great peaks on the other.

'I keep sinking about that creature who ran through us,' said Marine.

'Yes, so do I. It was the little hairy creature from the attic,' announced Jack.

'The hairy creature?' said Blue, 'From the attic? Oh per...lease!'

'You didn't see it!' retorted Jack.

'That noise was so peculiar,' remembered Marine 'It sounded so, vairy sad. What do you think it was 'Enri?' she asked their father.

'I've no idea but it made the hairs stand up on the back of my neck,' he replied.

'Oh well then, *definitely* Jack's hairy creature!' scoffed Blue.

Jack told Blue off under his breath.

'Perhaps it was a student dressed up?' suggested Dad. 'Whoever it was seemed to give Security the slip. I had thought for a horrible moment that we were all going to have to go flat on the floor whilst there was a shoot-out.'

'Oh! but now *you* are exaggerating,' said Marine.

Meaning that she thought I was exaggerating before, thought Jack, feeling frustrated. He knew what he had seen, but he also knew it sounded unbelievable.

It started to rain.

'Rain here means snow higher up,' said Dad cheerfully. This brightened up the atmosphere in the car.

It was getting dark. The great mountain shapes outside reminded Jack of his first impression of the hooded shape at the airport.

Droplets of rain ran past the window and he watched them catch up with other drops, until they doubled in size and rushed off the glass in the slipstream. Dad concentrated on the road. Blue dozed and Marine picked away and brushed off lots of grey green mossy bits, or was it lichen, that were inexplicably caught on her trousers?

'Zees were clean zis morning,' she muttered.

'What darling?' asked Dad.

'Oh nuzzing,' answered Marine.

'Nearly there,' said Dad to a sleeping Blue and Jack who had disappeared into his sister's iPad.

It was late before they finally found their hotel. Its roof was weighed down by a covering of a metre of snow getting higher every second as snow fell fast from the night sky. Christmas lights framed the door. As they stumbled up the path dragging their luggage, Marine playfully threw a snowball at their father. This was all the cue Blue and Jack needed - snowballs flew everywhere and Blue shrieked loudly as she scooped snow from the back of her neck. In the ensuing ducking and weaving Jack's backpack burst open. Marine helped him shove the clothes back in. He picked it up and it felt considerably lighter. So much lighter that Jack scanned the snow again to check if everything had been picked up. But he could not see any missing bits. Frowning to himself he caught up with the rest of the family. They arrived at the hotel door happy and puffing out steam, as they caught their breaths.

Jack did not notice the curious footprints marking the snow near where his bag had opened. Nor did he see that the footprints were made by something that was almost invisible. But they all heard the great moan that came from the night.

'What was that?' exclaimed their father.

'It must be zunder or a storm coming,' shivered Marine. 'Quickly, let's go inside. Look 'ere comes my bruzzer to meet us.'

Indeed, on the other side of the glass door they could see a kindly-looking man, with one arm stretched high in greeting and the other grabbing the door to open it wide. Bruno, Marine's brother, gave them a warm welcome. He shook Jack's hand and to Blue's discomfort gave her a kiss on both cheeks.

He called for hot chocolate drinks for Jack and Blue and an Armagnac for their father, who looked delighted to meet Bruno.

The hot chocolates were delicious. They sat beside a real wood fire which was built on a big stone platform, under a huge chimney. The adults talked a mixture of French and English and Jack sipped his sweet chocolate. He began to feel extremely sleepy.

'But look the young man needs to be shown his room, I zink!' exclaimed Bruno.

They were shown the lift. Blue had reluctantly agreed to share with Jack as it was too expensive for her to have her own room. Henry picked up the bags and passed them into the lift.

'I can't believe I had to pay overweight on this one,' he said as he lifted Jack's backpack with one finger. 'Their scales must have been wrong. What a swizz.'

'I did say Dad that we weighed it at home,' repeated Jack.

The lift stopped and they found their rooms.

'Well goodnight you two, don't stay up too long.'

'Night-night!' they called.

'I can't wait for tomorrow,' said Jack sleepily.

'Nor me,' answered Blue.

'We're so lucky' he said.

'But I wish Mum was here,' said Blue.

'Marine hasn't been too yuk.'

'Huh,' said Blue, 'her brother is really creepy. I wish they were all English!' she went on miserably, 'Jack?' she asked suspicious that he was not listening.

But the only answer came was a deep breathing. Jack was dreaming of the mountains and great yeti-like creatures, some kind and some fierce, moving as a great force through the faults and fissures of timeless granite.

Chapter 2

Blue and Jack woke very early.

'I can't wait to get up!' cried Jack.

'Let's go and explore the hotel,' said Blue.

'Do you think we can?' asked Jack.

'Of course we can, and have breakfast. Marine said last night that would be alright.'

Blue opened the curtains.

The light shocked both of them.

Then Blue sang, 'Ah, ah…ahh…ahhhh. Every inch of me is trembling, but not from the cold!'

Jack laughed. Blue was inclined to break into songs from 'Frozen' when she was particularly happy. He joined her at the window. Right before his eye the mauve mountain peaks were being lit up by the rising sun. A streak of light kissed the magnificent goose down duvet of snow before them.

An animal had left delicate blue-grey footprints that led into the wood close by. The topmost branches of the pine trees jauntily carried several centimetres of snow perched in their needles.

'It's a dream world,' breathed Blue.

'And we're going to be in it!' yelled Jack.

They dressed more quickly than they had ever done before and slipped out of their rooms. They took the stairs to the ground floor. There was a comfortable seating area with one old man reading a newspaper. He nodded at them, 'Bonjour' he said.

'Bonjour!' answered Jack and Blue caught unawares.

'That's the last French word I'm speaking though,' muttered Jack to Blue.

'Don't be so unsophisticated, you know what they say, when in Rome?'

'And I'm not speaking Italian either,' said Jack.

They paused outside the dining room. One couple was sharing a crumbly croissant in the corner.

'Do we dare go in?' whispered Jack. Blue hesitated.

'Excusez-moi,' they heard behind them. They moved to one side to let a waiter go through. He was only a year or two older than Blue and he carried an elegant coffee pot. As he moved through the door, he held it open.

'Ma'moiselle,' he said indicating to Blue to go through. So into the dining room they went.

The young waiter served coffee and then returned to them, 'Quel numero?' he asked indicating that he wanted to see their key number.

'Numero onze,' answered Blue.

The waiter checked his list and with an 'Ah bon!' he led them to a table for four by the window.

Jack nudged Blue, 'Do you think we should wait for Dad and Marine?' he asked quietly.

'I don't know how to say that,' replied Blue. 'Anyway they'll probably be ages, and I have never seen Marine eat breakfast.'

'Que voulez-vous boire?' asked the waiter. Blue blushed, this was suddenly more than her French could cope with.

'What would you like to drink, coffee … tea?,' translated the waiter, seeing her hesitate.

Blue blushed again, how stupid she felt not to have understood him the first time.

'Some coffee please,' she answered, surprising Jack. To his certain knowledge Blue had never drunk coffee.

'I'd like some tea,' he said. He was not absolutely sure that the waiter had heard him; he seemed to be concentrating entirely on Blue.

'I'd like some tea!' he repeated a little louder this time.

'Bien sur young sir,' said the waiter, but he sounded as though he was teasing Jack, rather than being respectful.

'Please 'elp yourself to the buffet,' said the waiter courteously to Blue, indicating a table covered with all manner of goodies.

'Merci,' replied Blue, 'Pierre,' she added softly reading his name off his label.

'Mercy, Pierre,' Jack mimicked her when Pierre was out of sight, 'And since when did you drink coffee?'

'Everyone in France drinks coffee; it's so English to drink tea.'

'What's wrong with being English?' asked Jack, his eyes round with amazement at the way his sister seemed to have changed out of all recognition.

'Dad's here!' exclaimed Blue, ignoring him.

Marine and their father were making their way across the restaurant. Occasionally Marine stopped to talk to people who were having breakfast. She seemed very much at home.

'Well, how about this?' greeted Dad, indicating the fabulous view from the window. 'Isn't it fantastic?'

'I can't wait to get out there Dad.'

'Well we've got to hire our skis and board, and get ski passes, but that shouldn't take too long. I think we can do most of it from here. Why don't you two get ready?'

'Don't worry, we will be right after you!' laughed Marine, who could see the impatience on their faces.

Hiring the snowboard and skis was a very exciting moment. There was a young man called Connor, who also came from the same country as the Snow Dome teacher - New Zealand.

He produced some lovely wide skis for Blue.

'These will be perfect for the new snow Blue.'

'Henry, I can recommend these,' he said to their father pulling out some more wide skis.

'Yes, they look great. But more importantly these boots feel surprisingly comfortable,' said their father, bending and flexing his knees as he tested his boots.

'If you want comfortable boots, you have to take up boarding. What are those like Jack?' asked Connor, indicating the rental boots that Jack was trying.

'Really nice,' agreed Jack.

But finding the right board for Jack was more difficult, as Connor sorted through the boards he commented, 'This one is too long,' or, 'That one is too tricky,' or, 'Too pretty, for a young man.' He hesitated, his head cocked as though he was listening and then he pulled a board out of the rack and looked at it with surprise.

'Yeees, I'd forgotten I had this board, our rep brought it in yesterday. It's the only one like it in the whole of the Trois Vallées, brand new, never been used…'

He brandished the board which was blue as the sky they could see out of the window. As he held it up they could see a curious and intricate design, which combined mountains with paths, and writings which were indecipherable. There were little drawings too, that reminded them of ancient Egyptian.

It was perfect.

'You should be able to *really* fly with this one,' said Connor.

'Not too literally I hope,' laughed Dad.

'Now I think you've got everything… Do you need sunscreen, extra scarves, anything else? It's really cold out there, I can recommend these hand warmers.'

Marine bought some hand warmers. These were little packets of chemicals that when you opened and shook them together, made a delicious heat.

'Anything else?' asked Connor. 'Ok. Have a great day!' He waved them off, and they traipsed out of the shop dragging skis and board, trying not to drop gloves and clumping along in their boots.

Dad had picked up their ski lift passes from Reception. 'These cost a bomb, look after them,' he warned them handing a small plastic card to both Blue and Jack.

'Put eet in a pocket on your left 'and side, and then the machine can scan eet easily and you can pass through the lift,' explained Marine.

They all did as Marine told them. Finally equipped, they were able to take the first steps onto the bottom of the ski slope and make their way across the white expanse to where a queue was forming, at the bottom of a chair lift.

The lift took at least six people. As the family lined up, they looked with horror at the speed in which the chair lift came rushing towards them. Surely it would knock them over or bang the backs of their legs? But thankfully at the last minute the machinery changed gear and slowed down, coming comfortably under their bottoms and scooping them up.

'Just how do I get off, if it goes that fast at the top?' gasped Jack.

'Don't worry, it goes precisely at the right speed when we are arriving,' Marine told him.

Somewhat reassured Jack could enjoy the glorious sensation of being carried up over the trees in the bright sunlight.

Here and there below, they noticed hare footprints and behind the hare footprints came ominous fox paw prints. They could even see where the fox had stopped to take a pee.

'That's why you don't want to eat yellow snow!' joked Dad.

Further up they began to see that where the trees were thinner and through the trees, there was a boarder making his way amongst them. He seemed only a little older than Blue. He was carving great rhythmic turns. It looked as though he was water skiing as behind him the snow sprayed out in an arc. He carried his arms out for balance and was going so fast that when he skied over a white hummock he would leave the snow and fly.

'He's like an angel!' gasped Blue, wondering if it was Pierre.

'He's a fantastic boarder,' agreed Marine.

Jack could not reply, the butterflies in his stomach were beginning to feel more like vampire bats.

'We're arriving,' warned his father. They made sure that they lifted the bar in front of them.

'Not too quickly, so 'igh up!' cried Marine. 'I 'ate it when I have no bar and I am still swinging up in space, I feel I want to jump off!'

They seemed to be hurtling awfully fast towards the place where they had to get off.

But the lift slowed down just at the last moment. Even so, Jack was taken by surprise at how difficult it was to transfer his weight onto the flat board on such a very slippery surface. It was only Marine's strong arm under *his* arm that helped him to keep upright and slide out of the way of the next people arriving fast behind them. He swerved to one side and promptly fell on his knees, very relieved that he was not mangled in the ski lift machinery, or still on the chair on the way back down again.

For a few moments they tried to get their bearings. Henry peered at the ski map, 'I think we will ski towards the hotel as it is a green run and everyone can see how they are going to get on before we tackle anything steeper.'

'Good idea 'enri,' agreed Marine.

'Go on Marine, show us the way,' encouraged their Dad.

Marine smiled at them all and asked, 'Ready?'

'Ready!' they all agreed in excited unison.

Marine made five careful but very neat turns. Blue followed tentatively holding her poles awkwardly in front of her. She managed to catch up with Marine. Dad and Jack cheered. Marine grinned at Blue and Blue could not help but give her a delighted smile back. Then Dad followed looking rather untidy and quite a lot faster. Disaster followed as he braked into Marine who dropped on top of him.

''enri, 'enri!' admonished Marine, but Jack was relieved to see that she was laughing.

They sorted themselves out and now it was Jack's turn. He inched forwards and took some speed. He crouched over his board and relaxed, as he had practised. His first sensation was that snow from the sky was very different from the snow in the Snow Dome. His board made a lovely noise as if it was humming. He changed his weight and direction. Everything worked perfectly. He was boarding on real snow on a real mountain! To people watching he was not going at any speed, but to Jack it felt as though he was whizzing along. Like the boy they had seen earlier in the woods, he could not help letting out a whoop of joy.

'Keep going, keep going, that eez sensational Jack, keep going. We are coming after you!' called out Marine. And it was true, instead of last, he was now leading the group. He glimpsed his family getting their act together so that they could catch up. He laughed as on he went, one linked turn after the other. He could do it! He could do it! It was totally awesome. To stop, he caught an edge and sat down hard.

His father arrived rather breathless. Marine and Blue, the latter not so tentative now, stopped with neat little turns. They had a self-congratulatory moment. It gave them a chance to look around and check where they were.

'Not far from the hotel,' said Dad.

'It is so beautiful today. We are very lucky to begin like this,' said Marine.

'Look at those peculiar marks in the snow!' said Blue pointing a few metres up the mountain.

'Yes! They sort of look like footprints,' said Dad.

'Maybe it's a yeti' laughed Blue 'and they go into the wood and don't come out.'

'They are absolutely extraordinary, they can't actually be footprints,' said Dad, his interest quickening. 'It must be a trick of the way the snow falls and the light ...' he squinted at the marks, '... or perhaps there are some odd shaped rocks underneath, that we can't see.'

'They are exactly like footprints, I can trace them all the way back to where Jack is sitting and then they go...' Blue squinted down the slope, 'They disappear where everybody else has skied,' she said disappointedly. 'I know Jack,' she laughed, 'it's your hairy monster.'

'Yeah yeah, very funny,' said Jack uncomfortably, he suddenly felt an inexplicable shiver of excitement or fear, and he heard his board vibrate and hum.

'What?' he exclaimed.

'What?' asked Blue and Dad back.

'My board - it makes the most peculiar noise,' said Jack

'Oh I know,' immediately agreed Marine, 'I 'ate the noise when it is be'ind me. It sounds so 'ow you say, 'arsh?'

'Harsh,' corrected Dad.

'But it is not a harsh noise, it's a sort of a sweet humming,' insisted Jack.

'You might think eets a sweet 'umming, but Jack I can assure you that when you 'ear the noise be'ind you, you feel like skiing very fast out of the way before someone comes crashing into you.'

'I can show you, listen,' said Jack peevishly, pushing himself up. 'Which way?'

'Just straight to the bottom,' said Dad.

Jack pushed off and was soon moving, but not so sweetly as before, and although he did not feel that he was losing his balance, he felt as though there was a weight on his board.

The others came past him calling out words of encouragement. He wanted them to hear the humming noise, but annoyingly the board sounded like all the other ski boards and he could no longer hear the humming. *It must have been a different type of snow,* thought Jack.

They did the same run twice more and every time Jack's board felt different to him; sometimes it hummed loudly and at other times he could hear nothing, especially, it seemed to Jack, when he went lower down the run.

Each time they had come down the run they had noticed a series of small hummocks in the snow. The third time they could see what they were for because experienced boarders and skiers were flinging themselves over the hummocks and doing jumps. One ski instructor landed and skied backwards for a few turns.

Their Dad called out jokingly, 'Let's leave the jumps for tomorrow.' But he clearly had no intention of trying them tomorrow, or at any other time.

'Oh Dad,' complained Blue, but she did not sound seriously put out either, tomorrow seemed quite soon enough to be jumping.

But Jack was so busy looking at one of the hummocks that he suddenly found himself on top of it. For a moment he was flying through the air, his arms outstretched and to everyone's surprise, including his, he landed upright and boarded on. Great shouts of congratulation came from his family and when they all finally stopped his Dad gave him a great hug and said, '*Really good* Jack,' making him feel warm inside.

Dad promptly called out, 'Lunch!' and Jack was sure that that morning had been the best of his life.

Chapter 3

They stopped for lunch in a charming wooden house right beside the piste.

'It's just like the travel brochure!' gasped Blue.

Marine told them her Great Aunt Tatine lived above the restaurant, but it was her grandson and his wife who ran the restaurant.

Although the sun was out, it was still incredibly cold.

'We eat inside today,' decided Marine.

As they stepped through the front door, heat from a log fire embraced them. The room smelt deliciously of hot sweet wine seasoned with cinnamon. The walls were lined with pine, stained dark brown from absorbing the smoke of hundreds of log fires.

Waiting inside was a woman who was no taller than Jack. Her face was covered with parallels of tiny lines, 'One for every blizzard I 'ave faced,' she liked to say. She had neat short grey hair and under her apron the children could see a bright red cardigan. She wore black laced leather shoes like the ones that men wear; her skirt was made of wool. She smiled delightedly at Marine.

'Tante Tatine!' cried Marine. There were lots of kisses and hugs for everybody. Jack felt his face grow hot at all the attention, especially as they were standing slap bang in the middle of a full restaurant. Then worse, Dad started talking in French. Jack squirmed.

'Dad's French is really good!' gasped Blue with admiration. Tatine showed the way to a table reserved for the family. Jack was relieved to find it was in the corner and not in the middle of the room.

The adults talked a mixture of French and English. 'It's called Franglais,' muttered Blue to Jack. But Jack was not listening, instead he was taking in all the decorations round him. Ancient tools and old farm machinery hung from the ceiling. His attention snagged on some objects that looked like tennis racquets without the handles, he had seen something looking exactly the same in Marines parent's attic.

Great Aunt Tatine saw Jack looking at them. 'They are snow shoes,' she told Jack. 'You fix them over your boots and you can walk on the deep snow.'

'We saw some prints a bit like that today,' said Blue.

'Prints? What ees this prints?' asked Tatine.

'Traces, Tante,' explained Marine 'They were big enough for snowshoes.'

'Except the footprints had toes,' corrected Jack, but immediately wished he had not opened his mouth.

'It's Jack's great monster with the hairy face, it's after him,' scoffed Blue.

'Dad thought they were like footprints!' retorted Jack.

'Well this is interesting!' exclaimed Tatine, 'My Grandmozzer used to see the Mountain People occasionally, and many times their traces, especially at night, and ooh la la the noise!' and to emphasize she slapped her two hands down on her knees.

'Oh no Tante, do not tell zem zees stories,' warned Marine 'we have 'ad enough of the furry mountain man!'

'But Marine,' admonished Tatine, 'my Grandmozzer was quite serious and everybody believed 'er - as I do.'

'Oh well, who knows?' answered Marine diplomatically.

'Jack had a nightmare all night,' laughed Blue, 'thinking about hairy monsters.'

'I did not!' said Jack indignantly.

'You did. You kept on yelling 'Help!' and 'Where are you?'

'I did not!' snapped Jack.

'Come on you two, that's enough. Let's drop it and decide what we're going to eat. Anybody for pommes frites?'

It was difficult to glower at Blue whilst eating the most delicious skinny chips and a nourishing burger. Anyway, Blue was busy glowering at Marine who had ordered veal.

'You can't eat veal. It's cruel!' gasped Blue when Marine ordered her lunch.

'It ees pink veal,' riposted Marine.

'What does that mean?' asked Jack.

''enri, please explain,' sighed Marine.

But Blue's father just laughed and said, 'I can't be bothered. We just have to agree to disagree.'

Blue looked as if she was going to take a breath and argue the point but something caught her eye and she stopped.

'What's that, in that photo?' she asked looking at the photo hanging on the wall.

'Ah ha, that is me when I was yong, and my familee, and my Grandmozzer on the right…' pointed out Tante Tatine and she took the sepia-coloured photo off the wall and handed it to Blue.

'And the little figure, is it a man or what, in a coat, on the right of your Grandmother? Look there?' pointed Blue, sounding excited.

'Where?' asked Tatine, who had taken down the photo and was peering at it. 'There is no one on the right.'

'Yes,' said Blue, 'right there … oh!' she squinted at the photo, 'but it's gone!' she exclaimed and studied the photo again… 'I saw, it looked just like, I don't know what?' and her voice faded and she looked rather pink, but she gave Jack what she hoped was a meaningful glance, but Jack was too busy chasing the last delicious chips round his plate and did not look up.

'Ah, here are your cokes,' said Henry, 'and a carafe of wine for the ladies,' he added, cheerfully pouring himself a glass after Tatine and Marine had refused. 'This should make our skiing *very* relaxed this afternoon. By the way, what do you think we should do this afternoon? Everyone's going so well perhaps we could venture a little further, what do you think darling?' he asked Marine.

Blue's face darkened when she heard the word 'darling' and Jack tensed up seeing Blue's glowering face.

I wish he wouldn't call her darling, thought Blue. It reminded her of Mum back at home. Blue felt angry and guilty at the same time. She felt angry because she still wanted her parents to be together, even though they argued all the time and were divorced. She felt guilty because sometimes she nearly admired Marine; she was so pretty and skied well, she made her father happy, but Blue felt she was not being loyal to her mother. Inadvertently she caught Tante Tatine's eye. Tante Tatine was watching her with a kindly expression.

'I 'ave the most delicious Tarte Myrtille, on the 'ouse, for the yong ones,' she announced and called the waiter over.

Tante Tatine was right, the little tarts, stuffed with tiny black berries and covered with whipped cream, were indeed delicious. Blue scraped away at the remnants of cream and deep purple myrtle berries, enjoying the pattern she was making on the plate. Her father and Marine lingered over their coffee. As she licked her spoon Blue found herself looking back at the photo across the table.

'May I see that again?' she asked her father. She was sure she could see the extra figure, but as her father reached for the photo the figure faded, so that by the time the photo was passed to Blue it was no longer there.

That is so peculiar, thought Blue, *creepy…*

Blue felt so confused about what she had seen, or what she had not seen, that it was a relief to get skiing again and just concentrate on the awesome sensation of floating over the wonderful snow.

That night Blue was impatient to share something with Jack, but she could not find the right moment.

Just as she started whispering to him her father came over to them.

'What are you on about?' asked Jack.

'Nothing,' she answered airily.

'Come on you two, we're going to play a game,' said Dad cheerily.

Then they all sat down and played a game that Marine taught them called Perudo.

'You shake your dice and hide them under your pot, so…' explained Marine.

'Someone starts and says that they 'ave, say, three threes'

'But we've got eight dice!' interjected Blue.

'Hang on Blue,' said Dad. He took over from Marine, 'The next person has got to go up more: they have to say they have 4 threes, or, three fives.' Blue and Jack looked at their father as if he was mad.

'Eventually the numbers become so big, you can challenge someone, and everybody has to show what they 'ave. If the person is right then the person 'oo did not believe them loses a life. If there are not enough numbers, then the ozzer person loses a life,' explained Marine. Blue and Jack looked blank.

'Oh! Let's just do it and it'll become clear,' said Dad.

The first few games did not really work, and then suddenly Jack and Blue got the message and started to enjoy the game. Just as Dad was challenging Blue, a mother and father and their daughter walked past.

'You sound as though you are having fun,' remarked the mother.

'Oh,' said Marine, who had met them earlier at breakfast. 'Please forgive me I 'ave forgotten your names. This is my partner 'enri and his son Jack and his daughter Sapphire.'

'Blue,' corrected Sapphire.

'I'm Lucy. This is my husband Mark, and our daughter, Melissa'

'Twiggy,' corrected Melissa.

Whilst the young fidgeted and tried to check each other out without appearing to look at each other, the adults engaged in animated chat. It was not long before they discovered that Mark, Twiggy's father, worked with Blue and Jack's uncle in London. Before they knew it, Marine had invited the family to join them in a game of Perudo.

Blue, Marine and Henry explained the game to Mark, Lucy and their daughter Twiggy. Luckily the new family had already played a version of Perudo, so they understood the very muddled and contradictory instructions.

Jack rather wished they had not come to join them as he was sure he would be out first. But in fact the game was more fun with extra people, except that, as Jack feared, he was losing dice quicker than anyone. He would have been out first, but then suddenly his father Henry, made all sorts of extravagant claims about which dice he was hiding under his own cup, and Henry was challenged so many times that it was he who was first out instead of Jack. *That's lucky,* thought Jack.

The evening was great fun and although Twiggy was younger than Blue, she and Blue were getting on really well.

'We should meet tomorrow?' suggested Marine. 'We could ski together?'

Oh no, thought Jack, *I bet we will hold them up.* A plan was made to meet at breakfast and see what the weather was like. It was quite late before everyone made their way upstairs saying good night to each other.

'Jack, I've been meaning to tell you about the photograph in the restaurant.'

'What?' said Jack, who was longing to go to sleep.

'I absolutely swear I saw a most peculiar figure in a hooded coat in the photo,' said Blue solemnly.

'Stop being mean Blue, I'm going to sleep,' said Jack, turning off the lights.

'No … I *really did* see something Jack,' said Blue.

Jack peered at her. He could vaguely see her face as she was backlit by the outdoor hotel lights.

'I still don't believe you.' But a note of interest crept into his voice.

'I don't care whether you believe me or not, but what I saw was this curious man with bare feet, he actually wasn't wearing shoes, in the snow.' To emphasize the point Blue repeated, 'He was standing in the snow without any boots and I promise you that when Tatine or whatever her name was, picked up the photo, the figure just faded away. I am not making this up, but the thing is Jack, it was *exactly* like that little figure you found in the attic!'

Jack felt a frisson of excitement, but he was not going to let Blue tease him again, he made a disbelieving noise.

'Well, I know what I saw,' insisted Blue.

'Well, *I* know what *I* saw,' said Jack, 'but you don't believe me and I don't believe you, so there. I just want to go to sleep. You're always teasing me, sometimes you can be pretty mean!'

'But I'm not being mean Jack, I'm agreeing with you. There's something very peculiar going on: we're being haunted by a furry creature!' hissed Blue.

Suddenly there was a knock on their door. Blue screamed and Jack jumped.

'Quiet you two or you will be too shattered to ski tomorrow,' called Dad.

Both Blue and Jack started to laugh quietly.

'I thought it was the yeti thing, coming to get us!' gasped Blue beginning to giggle hysterically.

'Shut up Blue, you're making too much noise, Dad'll be back!' said Jack, but he could not stop laughing either.

It was several moments before they stopped snorting with laughter.

Eventually Blue asked 'What did you think of Twiggy, Jack?'

'She seemed alright,' said Jack carefully.

'She could be your girlfriend and she's hardly a year older than you, her birthday's in January,' said Blue thoughtfully, who was always matchmaking with her girlfriends.

'What do you mean? I don't want a girlfriend, it's the last thing I want,' replied Jack scornfully. 'Go to sleep Blue, or Dad will be cross.'

Blue turned over.

After a moment a thought occurred to Jack. 'Blue?' he asked. But Blue had dropped off into a fitful sleep. Her legs twitched and she dreamt of coloured dice tumbling through the mountains and a furry creature who leapt in and out of ancient photographs.

Chapter 4

The next morning was as beautiful as the first. Blue and Jack were up quickly and went down to breakfast. Pierre looked pleased to see them and now that Blue had heard him talk English, she was reluctant to repeat the short phrases that she had tried yesterday other than a 'bonjour.'

They investigated the choices for breakfast deciding that the cheese and ham was a very odd choice and settled for muesli. Jack loved these moments when Blue was on his wavelength, and they could share the same ideas and tastes. They sat down in happy accord.

'Le sucre, jeune Jacques?' asked Blue passing the sugar.

'Oui, oui, ma soeur' replied Jack.

'Hi, morning you two, are your parents down yet?' asked someone. It was Mark from the evening before, with Twiggy.

'Not yet, but I expect they will be soon,' replied Jack

'Marine is NOT our mother,' pointed out Blue at the same time.

'Of course she isn't, my mistake,' said Mark cheerfully. 'We're meeting some friends for lunch today, and it is ski school for all of tomorrow, so we'll have to make another plan.'

'OK,' said Blue.

'See you later,' said Twiggy.

'Thank goodness,' breathed Jack, 'I don't want to ski with anybody else, it was such fun yesterday, I'd just like to do the same again.'

'I think it's a pity, I like Twiggy, I hope we are in the same class,' said Blue disappointedly.

Marine and Henry joined them. Henry had the ski map and Blue soon forgot her disappointment when he flattened the map on the table, and invited her to choose where they would spend the day.

'Let's go over a bit and then go down that run called 'La Truite'' she begged.

'What does that mean?' asked Jack

'The Trout,' answered Marine, 'Look it runs beside a stream, although I should imagine that this stream must be frozen solid absolutely. I wonder what the trout do?'

After breakfast they tramped out into the perfect morning. They all felt optimistic and excited.

Cheerful cries of, 'Salut!', 'Ciao!' and 'Hi!' could be heard everywhere.

'Now have you got everything?' Dad asked. 'Ski passes?' He had got into a habit of checking that nothing was forgotten. Their mother was completely scatty, she never had her purse and the car keys were always put somewhere different.

'Check,' replied all three.

'Hat and gloves?' he asked.

'No gloves!' wailed Jack.

'You'll have to go and get them,' insisted his father.

'Hurry up,' Blue groaned 'Why do you always forget something?'

'I don't need them,' said Jack, but he could feel the cold already biting at the tips of his fingers and as the rest of the family was insisting that he *did* need them, he was already placing his board against the hotel wall and moving towards the door.

His board seemed annoyed too; it was making a peculiar hum. As he moved away, he thought *wait a minute how can it be making a noise?* But as he moved back towards the board, everyone yelled at him again.

'Hurry up JACK!'

To go back to his room meant that Jack had to take his boots off in the boot room. There were rules about not walking inside the hotel with outdoor shoes on. He dashed upstairs found his gloves under a mound of bed clothes and ran down the stairs quickly.

When he got back outside feeling hot in his boarding gear, he expected rude comments about how long he had taken, but Blue, Dad and Marine were staring at his board which was now upside down on the snow.

'Jack your board just shot into the sky and somersaulted backwards!' yelled Blue as he arrived.

'I've never seen anything like it,' said Henry, 'the bindings must have been pressed against the balcony and created a peculiar force on the board.'

'You cannot imagine 'ow it made me so frightened; it was leaping in the air,' added Marine.

Jack picked up his board rather gingerly.

'Well it's alright now,' he reassured them, putting his arms round it. 'Let's go?'

'Has everyone got their mobiles?' asked Dad.

'Yes,' said Blue impatiently.

'Jack?' asked Dad.

At this point Jack felt he had to lie because his father had given him his mobile when he had left his Mum. 'Something to keep in touch with,' his father had said, 'You can text me anytime you feel like it, old man.'

Jack slapped his pocket and said 'yes' firmly. Blue frowned, Jack had told her the story and Blue had insisted that he told a teacher. But before Jack had plucked up the courage to admit that he had had a mobile at school, the term had ended. Blue knew this was not the time to challenge Jack, there would be a row and that would spoil the day.

Satisfied with Jack's reply, his father said cheerfully, 'Allons-y,' and they all clumped towards the queue which was forming at the bottom of the fast chair lift.

'I love this bit!' yelled Blue as they were scooped up into the sky swinging through the trees. Snow floated off their boots and their breath fogged up their goggles and glasses.

'I think it must have snowed again last night. All yesterday's tracks are covered up and the trees have an extra icing,' pointed out Dad.

'We 'ave the good luck, but 'ow cold it ees!' gasped Marine.

Blue agreed and for a split second she wished that it was she who was snuggling into a wide furry collar.

At the highest point from the ground, the lift came to a sudden jolting and unexpected stop.

'What's happened?' gasped Jack. 'We're not going to be here for ever, are we?'

'Of course not!' laughed Dad, 'They're probably helping a child on, or there has been a temporary stop of electricity. Nothing to worry about.'

'Last year,' began Blue, who liked to boast a little bit about her school skiing week. 'The lift stopped for so long that our teachers organised a sing song and we sang rude limericks about each other. I'd just thought of a really good one for Mrs Brown, when it started again.'

'I 'ate it when we are left 'anging in space, you know 'ow I don't like eet,' moaned Marine. But just then their lift juddered once and then continued smoothly up the mountain until it arrived at the top and Dad began to raise the bar.

'Not so fast, 'enri, not so fast,' admonished Marine.

At last they were all ready for the first run of the day.

'Right. This time only halfway down, and then we branch off at the lift on the right. Got it you lot?' demanded Henry as he started off. 'Make sure you don't miss it.'

In their own ways they skied and boarded down the slope.

How brilliant to be on my board again, thought Jack, *I really love you board!* he thought to himself, and the board hummed back to him. He hoped that Blue would hear it, but he was no longer going to point it out to her as he did not want to be teased.

The next lift was only a two-seater. Blue stopped chatting to him to point out a group of people on the slope below.

'I wonder if that is Twiggy?'

'Where?' asked Jack.

'She's with about five people, and she's wearing exactly the same hat. I saw her this morning, she waved at me,' said Blue.

'It could be,' agreed Jack. They watched the small figure boarding nicely down the slope.

'She's not going any faster than you,' said Blue loyally.

'She's miles better than me,' said Jack modestly, but he stared hard at the small figure, and wondered how he would be able to cope on the run - it looked pretty steep.

The lift they were on was an old-fashioned type that hardly slowed down at the top. It delivered them onto an icy patch without ceremony. Jack had to concentrate hard to get his balance. Then he had to do bunny hops to join Blue.

'That's the most difficult bit!' he gasped.

Now they skied into a different valley.

'This is the valley of Courchevel,' their father told them. The first bit was not so difficult, but there were many more people skiing on it than the family were used to.

'We 'ave arrived with the world,' announced Marine rather gloomily.

'Someone only just missed me!' gasped Blue, 'It was a boarder going flat out!'

'Ah zees boarders,' agreed Marine, 'always they are so dangerous!'

'Not Jack?' challenged Blue.

'No,' agreed Marine hurriedly, 'Jack 'ees a most considerate boy on a board.'

Their little party moved off carefully and after they had joined a path the slope opened out to an area where there were more lifts.

'Let's just keep going!' called Dad, as he whizzed past them. The slope flattened out but flowed along like a great benign roller coaster. Just as they picked up too much speed the slope would rise again and they would regain control, just as they slowed almost to a halt, then they would reach the rise and plummet down again.

'This is awesome!' shrieked Blue.

'Wahoo!' Jack yelled back.

Eventually they reached a large mountain village to the left. Directly in front of them was a range of cable car lifts going in every direction.

'It's like the market on Saturday mornings!' exclaimed Blue.

'Busier…' added Henry.

'We can ski on through 'Enri,' pointed out Marine. 'If we continue, we can bypass this place and go somewhere lower and per'aps a little quieter.'

They perused the ski map.

'This way,' said Dad and he led the way through a snowy tunnel under one of the buildings.

Jack had to take one leg out of his bindings and scooter along the flat tunnel, which was hard work, but it was worth it when he was presented with another enticing ski slope, studded with trees.
They came to a stop when they saw lots of people tobogganing. It looked fantastic fun.

'Can we do that?' asked Blue eagerly.

'Yes, we can drive round one evening,' agreed Marine.

They skied a little further and Dad spied a restaurant on the side of the slope.

'I'm ravenous!' he announced and no one disagreed.

'I love chips, they're my favourite thing ever,' pronounced Jack, as he squeezed tomato ketchup all over his heaped plate. Their father had chosen a sausage which was a suspicious grey colour and when he cut it open, squiggly things, that had been kept back by the tight casing, leapt out.

'Yeurgh!' said Blue and Jack simultaneously.

'I could never eat that in a million years,' said Jack seriously.

'Get on with your own food, this sausage is delicious' said their father manfully shovelling up another mouthful of unidentifiable parts of a pig.

For the rest of the afternoon the foursome explored the Courchevel valley, it seemed that it was covered with lifts going in every direction.

'We 'ave ardly touched the area,' said Marine loftily when Blue exclaimed over the amount of runs there were to do.

'Let's do a different valley every day?' suggested Jack.

'That's a good idea Jack,' agreed his Dad.

When they got back to the hotel in the evening everyone declared that it had been the best day *ever*. As Jack ran upstairs jauntily, he replayed every wonderful moment. Feeling completely elated he bounced around the corner and ran straight into … Nasty Nick from his school!

Jack was so horrified that he actually yelped.

Nasty Nick looked briefly nervous too, probably remembering that he had swiped Jack's mobile, but he recovered his composure quickly.

'Are you staying here?' he asked Jack.

'Yes, I am' replied Jack miserably.

'You little toe rag, you just keep out of my way, do you understand?' demanded Nick.

Jack longed to say, '*You* keep out of my way, I got here first.' But even as he was thinking this, the word that came out of his mouth was, 'Yes.'

'Yes what?' demanded Nick.

'Yes, I'll keep out of your way,' replied Jack sullenly. Nick leered at him, the lift arrived and thankfully he got into it. Jack scuttled upstairs, but he had only taken one step when he met Twiggy. She looked aghast.

'Who was that?' she asked. 'How can he tell you to keep out of his way?'

'He's a bloody awful bully. Everybody hates him' said Jack embarrassedly. He wished fervently that Twiggy had not heard.

'I hate people like that. We must plot something to make him sorry,' she said clenching her fists. This was a new experience for Jack; last term when he was being bullied all the others melted away. But Twiggy looked fierce and determined, more importantly she seemed to be on Jack's side.

'I was coming to ask if you and Blue would like to meet me and hang out?' she asked.

Jack felt confused, one moment it was his best day ever, just now he discovered Nasty Nick in his hotel which was his worst nightmare and now this fit girl was on his side and inviting him (and admittedly his sister too) to hang out with her.

'We saw you boarding today, you go really fast,' he said.

'Oh! I don't' said Twiggy blushing, she went on, 'Are you going to ask your sister?'

'OK, but she might be sleeping, she said she was knackered when she got back.'

'Text me,' said Twiggy, getting out her mobile.
'I can't. That piece of . . .' he indicated where Nasty Nick had gone, '. . . nicked it off me last term.'

'We'll bury him,' announced Twiggy seriously. 'Ring my room number. Its 321. Ok?'

'Ok!' Jack agreed and Twiggy ran on, up another flight of stairs.

Jack went toward his room, but the further he went away from Twiggy and her fearless determination, the more miserable he felt, and as he walked into his room he felt as low as he had at school, and as helpless.

'I wish you had your own key so I didn't have to get up to let you in,' said Blue peevishly as he arrived.

Miserably Jack swore at her. Blue looked at him in astonishment.

'Keep your hair on Jack. Dad would be furious if he heard you. What's bugging you?'

'Everything. You know that boy who stole my mobile?'

'Nasty Nick? Yes?'

'He's staying in this hotel,' said Jack miserably.

'How do you know?'

'I just bumped into him.'

'What did he say?'
'He told me to keep out of his way'

'What did you say?'

And here Jack had to swallow an ache in his throat. He felt as if the wonderful holiday had come to an end.

'Well, I said I would,' spat out Jack ashamed.

Although Blue often bickered with Jack, she was very fond of him. She knew he was a kind and generous sort and to see him looking so miserable and trying not to cry, made her feel outraged.

'We'll get him,' she promised. 'I'll think of something, even if we have to tell Dad.'

'If you tell Dad I'll never speak to you again. He's bound to tell off Nasty Nick's Dad and then I'm finished!' cried Jack bitterly.

'OK, keep a lid on it Jack, but I'm not going to let him ruin our holiday, OK?'

There was silence.

'OK Jack?' insisted Blue.

'What can you do? I'm finished,' stated Jack.

'Don't be silly Jack. I'll think of something to serve him right.'

'That's what Twiggy said.'

'Twiggy? Have you seen Twiggy?' asked Blue.

'Oh yes, I almost forgot, she asked us to hang out, room number 321. You've got to ring her.'

'321?' repeated Blue as she picked up the hotel phone.

She dialled the number and was soon speaking to Twiggy, 'Come on let's go up to her room now,' she said.

'You're lucky to have a room to yourself,' said Blue as soon as she saw Twiggy's room. Twiggy's room looked towards the ski slope. The moonlight caught the ski lift mechanism and made the trees look black, their shadows extending onto the slope.

'The moon doth shine as bright as day,' quoted Twiggy.

'So that's why we learn nursery rhymes,' laughed Blue.

'I feel like going out and chucking snowballs,' said Jack.

'Too cold!' shouted the girls in unison.

It was a really nice evening. The girls had a tacit understanding to stop Jack feeling miserable and they laughed together as they made more and more fantastical plans to deal with Nasty Nick, in wonderfully gruesome ways.

Eventually Twiggy's father came upstairs. He had been in the bar of the hotel.

'Good Lord, aren't you lot in bed by now? Time to hit the sack!'
'Dad, can Blue share with me?'

'That would be fantastic! Can I?' added Blue excitedly.

'You'd have to ask your father Blue. I certainly can't speak for him, but I know Twiggy's Mum wouldn't mind and it doesn't make any difference to me.'

Blue rang her father's hotel room and they had a short discussion in which Blue said things like, 'No, Jack won't mind,' and, 'No, of course we won't talk all night.' The matter was agreed and Blue dashed downstairs to get her things.

'You don't mind Jack, do you?' asked Twiggy thoughtfully.

'No, of course not' said Jack stoutly. But he *did* mind, he had enjoyed having Blue for company. She made him feel safe.

'Will you wake me when you go down for breakfast?' he asked Blue.

'Of course, you don't mind Jack, do you?' she asked again somewhat guiltily. Jack reassured her and wandered downstairs rather dejectedly. Who should he meet but Nasty Nick?

'Loser!' hissed Nasty Nick as Jack tried to slip past him.

'Nicky?' questioned a woman coming up behind.

'Not you!' said Nick.

'Well who were you talking to, my boy?' as she passed Jack he smelt strong perfume, smoke and alcohol. He did not hear Nasty Nick's answer as just behind Nasty Nick's mother came Marine.

'Pah!' she exclaimed waving her hand in front of her face. 'I sink zat lady 'as been 'aving too good time.' She went on, 'I 'ear zat Blue is sharing with Twiggy. It ees nice for two girls to share, but you don't mind Jack?'

'It was nice having Blue with me, but I know she didn't want to share with me really, so it's better this way,' he said.

Marine gave him a short hug. 'You are a vairy sympathetique boy Jack, I am glad we are skiing togezzer.' She hesitated, 'I expect you miss your Mama. I hope you tell 'er about 'ow well you are going?'

'I don't but Blue does,' answered Jack.

'And why don't you do also?'

'Because someone nicked my mobile off me at school, and that very person is staying in this hotel. You just missed seeing him, that was his mother you came up the stairs behind. He's the school bully; everyone hates him!'

'Well I 'ate 'im too in this case,' pronounced Marine. 'I will ask his muzzer to demand your mobile back right now.'

Stricken with horror Jack realised that this was the last thing in the world he wanted to happen. Marine looked at Jack's expression and led him to his room.

'Sit down Jack,' she patted the space beside her on the bed.

But before she could speak, Jack gasped, 'Marine you must swear that you will never ask his mother about my mobile. If you do he will beat me up and make my life at school an absolute misery.'

'Non, non Jack, I am sure we 'ave to discuss thees with 'ees mozzer,' insisted Marine. But as looked she looked at Jack she could see he was deadly serious.

'Please, please Marine don't do that. You don't know his friends, they'll get me!'

Marine shook her head. 'As you ask me Jack, I will not betray you, but I think zis is the wrong action and it is necessary to stand up to the bully of the world. Per'aps 'ee is un'appy and 'ee is undernees it all perfectly charming.'

''ee' said Jack now dropping his aitches as he was so caught up with communicating with Marine the seriousness of the situation, ''ee is absolutely and completely *not* charming.'

'Well, we will see. I will sink 'ow I am going to make a plan, and we *will* get your mobile back.'

'That's going to be impossible Marine – you won't tell anyone will you, especially Dad?'

'This is what I always say: no yong person should have zings that are expensive, because they only cause trouble and worry,' said Marine.

She grabbed his hands and gave them a squeeze.
'Jack you must worry no longer, you must enjoy your 'oliday. We will not let the school bully spoil your time. He will not win in the end I assure you. Promise me that you will worry no more?'

She looked him in the eyes, 'Promise me?' she insisted.

'I promise,' replied Jack dutifully.

'And you will go to bed now because it is late and we will 'ave a marvellous day tomorrow. You must promise this too.'

'I promise,' said Jack looking more cheerful.

Marine kissed him on both cheeks and said, 'Good night.'

As Jack settled himself under his duvet he was aware of the silent bed next to him. But he felt a little more cheerful. It was true: a problem shared was a problem halved, it was what his mother always said.

Suddenly the hotel telephone shrilled. It must be Blue ringing to say goodnight.

'Hello,' he answered.

'Hello,' Nick's voice mimicked him. 'Sleep well, loser.'

Jack slammed the telephone down hard.

It beeped again.

'Go AWAY!' he yelled and put the receiver down and then picked it up so that the person on the other end would get the engaged signal. His heart was thudding. A few moments later he got out of bed and tested that his door was locked. Then he got back into bed and watched the phone with the receiver off the hook for a while. Then he turned over and at last his heart stopped beating quite so fast. He sighed miserably and a dreamless sleep overcame him.

Chapter 5

Ski school was due to start the following morning and Jack woke to a third fine day. Blue had been to ski school the year before and had made good friends, so she was eager to join. Jack was not so easily convinced, for one thing he would not be in the same class as Blue, as she skied and he boarded.

He dressed quickly and hearing no answer from Twiggy's room when he rang her room number, he went downstairs to see if they were already up.

Downstairs he scanned the dining room quickly to see if Nick was there but was very relieved when instead of Nick, he saw Twiggy and Blue wave him over to their table. Both parents were late rising so the three of them had a cheerful breakfast, with both girls practising French with the waiter Pierre, and even Jack tried out some phrases with an exaggerated French accent. The odd thing was, the more he exaggerated, the more Pierre seemed to understand.

Eventually Henry their father arrived without Marine. Henry seemed worried.

'Marine has a problem at work, so we may have to go home early,' he said.

Blue and Jack looked horrified.

'Don't worry, if that happens, I've spoken to Twiggy's parents and they have kindly said that they could look after you, but I'm not sure your Mum would like that as she hasn't met them and doesn't know how nice they are,' this with a smile towards Twiggy, 'and I don't want to ring her too early.'

'Mum won't mind,' said Jack and Blue together.

'Well, we'll see. It might be able to be sorted from here, or I might not be needed too. Anyway let's not worry yet.' He sat down and asked Pierre for a quick coffee. 'We mustn't be late for ski school.'

Getting to ski school entailed catching the lift down to a different valley.

At the ski school gathering point, there was a collection of excited people of all ages. Jack's heart sank when he saw one of them was Nick. He could hear Nicks father's voice coming across the slope. He was a large man and he loomed over the ski instructor, as he boomed at him various directives.

Everybody heard him say, 'My boy is very capable, he should be in the improvers class.' They could not hear the ski instructor's reply but they could easily hear Nick's father - words like, 'boring' and, 'I insist,' punctuated the pristine alpine air.

Henry stared in the direction of the raised voice.

'Isn't that man in our hotel?' he asked. 'He sounds perfectly awful.'

Twiggy looked and whispered something to Blue; she in turn asked, 'Is that nasty Nick?'

'Yes, it is. If he's in my class, I'm not going,' muttered Jack. The girls nodded sympathetically.

'I don't blame you,' agreed Twiggy fiercely.

Twiggy moved off towards her class, and Jack saw his father talking to a cheerful-looking ski instructor holding a snowboard. He called Jack over.

'Olivier, this is my son Jack.'

Olivier stuck out a hand, and in an accent exactly like Marine's said, 'Welcome Jack, I 'ear that you 'ave 'ad some experience, but not much so I sink you can begin 'ere until we see what you can do. Some of the class are experienced skiers, but trying snowboard for the first time, and some are like you, who 'ave 'ad some lessons where you can practise boarding indoors, so I zink that we 'ave a class that are much the same standard.'

Jack felt reassured, especially as he could see a class who were moving off where one of figures was Nick. Jack felt overwhelmed with relief, but at the same moment with a sinking heart he recognised another figure in the same class: it was Twiggy. Today Twiggy had given up her board and was on skis.

'Allons-y mes braves!' called out Olivier and his class of seven trooped off.

In Jack's class there were three friends of about seventeen who joked together and did not take much notice of the rest. There was an Italian boy of about his age and two girls slightly older. The girls, whose names were Lorelei and Ellie inevitably bonded, leaving Jack with the Italian boy. His name was Benito. Easy to remember, like my best friend Ben, but with a little bit extra, Jack thought to himself.

They started on the nursery slope just to see whether they could remain upright or turn at all. Jack's board seemed very sluggish but he managed all the moves that Olivier asked for. Everyone got going quite quickly but on the nearly flat slope it was difficult to see exactly how good anyone *really* was. After half an hour, Olivier decided that they were certainly capable of sitting on a chair lift and going somewhere a lot higher and a little more challenging.

The three older boys got on a lift before Jack and Benito, followed by the girls and Olivier. They travelled over the trees and up the mountain. As they arrived at the top they could see pretty good carnage: the older boys had been teasing each other and as a joke one pushed the other two as they were getting off, leaving the next people faced with a hazard of fallen bodies.

The lift operator, seeing that the next chair of people would be deposited on top of the boys, stopped the lift and started yelling at the teenagers in various languages, leaving Benito and Jack with all the other passengers swinging backwards and forwards in the sky. They could not resist laughing as they watched the boys on the ground shuffle and heave themselves out of the way, with the lift operator still telling them off.

After a word of caution from Olivier off they started again. There were lots of falls including Jack who managed to board into Ellie. It was fun and time passed quickly. At last it was time to snowboard the whole slope back to the meeting place. The last bit was much steeper and here the class divided. The older boys fell everywhere usually accompanied with good-natured swear words and 'man' and 'hung over'. The girls inched along, not falling but going very carefully indeed. When it was Benito's turn, he went pretty well.

Then it was Jack's turn. He found the sight of so many of his class either sitting on the ground or moving so cautiously, off-putting. He set off very carefully, but his board felt lighter and it made a sweet humming noise. Jack relaxed and shifted his weight to turn. The board seemed to know the perfect line, he travelled through the fallen class as they gazed at him with some admiration. Triumphantly he came to a halt next to Olivier.

'Eh bien, that was vairy good, vairy good, you are the champion of the class, bien, bien, now I 'ave to persuade the ozzers to find a good way down.'

'Well done board!' said Jack to the board feeling slightly ridiculous but also delighted at the same time. How could he be talking to a snowboard? He really felt that its peculiar hum meant that it was communicating to him.

He had to wait sometime before Olivier cajoled the girls to be a little braver and redemonstrated the right technique to the older boys.

'Man, that was hard,' said Toby, one of the older boys Eventually everyone arrived at the bottom and said, see you tomorrow to Olivier. He gave a thumbs up to Jack and happily Jack took off his board and walked over the flat meeting area to where he could see his father.

'How was that?' asked Henry.

'Fantastic!' enthused Jack.

'Great!' responded his father. 'Let's eat. Blue and Twiggy are over there. We'll catch that bubble car and meet everybody at the top to have a bite.'

They had a bit of a queue to catch the bubble car, it fitted eight. It was the first time Jack had been on one and it had the feeling of a fairground ride about it.

'How was your class Jack?' they all wanted to know. Jack described his morning. Blue too had good stories to tell but Twiggy was feeling very indignant.

'Nick is *so* superior and he doesn't really ski that well, but he has skied *everywhere,* in the States, Canada, Italy, and Spain. He just boasts and boasts, and mostly he talks *at* Cyrille, that's our ski instructor. I'm sure he is boring him as much as he is boring us,' but Twiggy had not finished, 'and he makes excuses: if he falls over it's because his boots hurt, or someone was in his way, or the edges on his skis have not been sharpened properly. He's just one big loser.'

'Nick?' said Jack's father thoughtfully, 'I'm sure I've heard his name somewhere?'

'He's in our hotel,' said Blue and changing the subject, 'We're not going home early Dad, are we?'

'It's not decided yet,' said Henry, 'Marine has been on the computer all morning trying to work things out.'

He sounded rather worried and despondent, and Jack wished that Blue would leave the conversation alone, but she carried on, 'If you do decide to go home, can I ring Mum to ask if we can stay please?'

'Well if Twiggys' parents are OK with that, and it is asking a lot, then I'll let you ring her Blue. But you must tell her that I said it is entirely her decision. You know Mum, she'll feel that I am copping out of the responsibility of looking after you two reprobates,' he said giving Jack a hug to show he did not really mean that Jack was a reprobate. Actually, Jack was not entirely sure what a 'reprobate' was.

Blue was always more sparkly when Marine was not around and she made them all laugh with her tales of her class. They sat outside for the first time for lunch, as it was not nearly so cold.

'The wind is coming from a completely different direction,' pointed out Henry.

In the afternoon they skied towards the Méribel valley and down 'La Truite' again. Twiggy had popped into the hotel to swap her rental skis back to her board.

'What a treat to go down the Trout!' called out Twiggy playing with the words, as she boarded next to Jack. He could nearly keep up with her. The only thing was that her board seemed faster than his. His board sounded subdued, not like the happy hum he enjoyed higher up.

'What's the matter board?' asked Jack.

Later the girls nudged each other and laughed whenever he talked to his board.

'Laugh away, I don't mind,' he said. 'My board is a true friend.'

'*My* board is going to be called 'Wicked'' said Twiggy.

'I name my skis 'Swiftflight',' announced Blue joining in. 'That's what I would call a pony if I ever had one,' she explained to Twiggy. 'What about you Jack?'

'My board is called …' He was going to call his board Ben after his school friend but instead he found himself saying, '… Avalanche Rider.'

'Let's hope not,' laughed Dad. 'This run is quite exciting enough.' They raced down to the Place Centrale where everyone from Méribel met.

'Just time to catch the Rhodos lift. Hurry now,' called Dad. In fact, there was at least an hour, before the lifts closed.

'Perhaps we've got time to have a hot chocolate at Tante Tatine's restaurant?' suggested Dad.

'Ooh yes!' responded three keen voices.

'Can we have our usual table?' asked Blue.

'You've only been there once,' laughed Jack.

'I want to look at that picture again,' muttered Blue to Jack.

Luckily the table was free and Blue moved to see the photo. As she looked the expression on her face was amazed delight.
'See,' she said, 'I told you there was this figure,' and she took the photo from the wall to pass it over to Jack and Twiggy.

'That's my figure!' said Jack excitedly 'That's exactly what I told you. Now do you believe me?' and he began to tell Twiggy all about the little figure that he had found in the attic, and how it had changed into a great hairy figure. He described the huge noise that boomed about in the airport.

'Ok,' said Twiggy slowly extracting what sense she could from the garbled story, 'but how's that figure in the airport and now in this photo?' she could not keep disbelief out of her voice.

Dad came over having asked for the hot chocolates.

'What are you all looking at?'

'The Yeti,' replied Blue.

Dad looked, 'I think it's rather rude to describe Tante Tatine's husband as a yeti,' he spoke sharply.

'No, not the man next to Tante Tatine, Jack's figure right there,' said Blue jabbing at the photo with her finger, but as she did she stopped, frowning.

'I don't believe it, it's happened again, it's gone!' she gasped.

'So it has!' added Jack peering.

'Can I see?' asked Twiggy. 'That's odd,' she said doubtfully, 'I thought I saw a …' her voice trailed off as she tried to remember what exactly it was that she had seen…

'Ha ha, very funny,' said Dad sarcastically. 'Come on, drink up before the chocolate gets cold and then join me,' as he headed for the exit.

'It must have been a trick of the light or the candle shadow,' said Twiggy trying to understand. But Blue and Jack were having none of that; they gave each other meaningful looks across the table.

'Can I see the photo again?' she asked. But no amount of staring at the sepia photo would bring the figure back again.

'So Twiggy…' asked Blue eagerly 'What did you see?'

'I thought I saw a huge man-like thing,' said Twiggy, 'but obviously I was wrong.'

'It goes when an adult comes up to look at it,' insisted Blue.

'Blue don't be silly, how can that be?' scoffed Twiggy. 'I know it's really funny, but it's the light, it must be, think about it!'

'I've seen it *twice* and I don't care what you say, there is something really peculiar about that photo and it's definitely got nothing to do with the light,' replied Blue urgently.

'I know, let's not make any decisions until we see the photo just one more time,' said Jack quickly. He did not want the girls to argue.

'Fair enough,' said Twiggy, whilst Blue just harrumphed, annoyed. But at least the difficult moment was gone and when they got into the hotel Marine announced that unfortunately she *did* have to go back home, but before she went, she would take them all sledging this very evening.

'So, keep your warm clothes on,' she advised 'When 'enri has had a cup of tea we will all go out; drive down and around to the next valley and go down the toboggan run.'

A little later, they all clambered into Henry's hire car including Twiggy's parents.

'I'm sure this is illegal,' worried Henry as all the young had to sit on laps.

'Oh, it's not far,' laughed Mark and Lucy, Twiggy's parents. They seemed very chilled, *not a bit like Dad,* thought Jack.

The toboggan run was lit up with lights that disappeared down the hill and around the corner. There was rock music coming from huge speakers and above the music you could hear screams of excitement from people on their sledges, meeting the first corner at top speed.

At the top there was a delicious smell of Christmas: a stall was selling vin chaude, hot wine scented with cinnamon and nutmeg and sweetened with lots of sugar.

'I think we should have one of those darlings, don't you?' suggested Lucy.

Mark issued everyone with their toboggans.
'I'm taking a lift down to the end with Lucy and there's ten pounds for the first over the finishing line,' Mark announced.

Then to Blue and Jack's amazement Lucy handed them a plastic mug full of the steaming red drink.

'We call it Dutch courage, although I can't think why. My grandparents were Dutch and they were very brave, but they never drank alcohol. Don't worry it's not very strong,' she reassured Henry who was looking very disapproving.

Whilst Blue had often had sips of champagne at celebrations, Jack had never drunk anything alcoholic. Twiggy, however, seemed quite at home with her drink. It seemed rude to refuse, so Jack took a polite sip, it was exactly as he expected; a horrible mix of sweet and bitter, and he could not avoid making a face. He handed it to Blue, who seemed to have finished her first mug in record time.

'Look at him?' sneered a voice. 'Aren't you a little junior to be drinking alcohol? Don't you think you should leave that for the grown-ups?' remarked Nick sauntering past dragging a toboggan behind him.

Jack found himself unconsciously moving behind the girls. To his horror he heard Twiggy say hotly, 'Arrogant show-off!'

But Nick just made an ugly face and moved on to where his parents were talking to some other people. To his displeasure the other people were Henry and Marine and all of them seemed to be getting on fine.

'Last one lays the table for a week,' giggled Nick's mother as she moved off.

'Well, we know who that is going to be, don't we?' said Nick looking back at Jack. 'We know who is going to be the total loser?' he sneered.

'Probably you!' said Twiggy.

'Yeah, well try not to break a leg,' scoffed Nick looking at her menacingly.

'Are you coming Nicky?' called his Mother. 'Are your friends coming?'

'Go on Nicky,' urged Twiggy, 'Mummy's calling.'

Quick as a flash Nick picked up a lump of ice and threw it as hard as he could at Twiggy. It hit her full pelt in the face. She threw her hands to her face and gasped.

'You creep!' spat Blue.

Out of the corner of his eye Henry saw that Twiggy had been hurt. He came striding over.

'Hey young man, that was a stupid thing to do, you can hurt someone if you're not careful.'

'What's going on here?' asked Nick's father turning back.

Henry was looking at Twiggy's face. Jack could see that Twiggy was trying not to cry, but although it was quite dark, he could see the stall lights catching and illuminating the tears escaping from her eyes.

'It's just the shock,' she said defiantly.

'It's cut her face,' said Henry crossly to Nick.

'Now, now, I'm sure he didn't mean it You know the young, they love a snowball fight,' said Nick's father.

'She needs a moment. Why don't you go on?' replied Henry.

Nick's father turned away sulkily. Nick's mother, Marine and Twiggy's parents had already moved off to catch the lift which would take them down to the finish of the toboggan run.

As Nick and his father made their way towards the start, Jack saw Nick's father give Nick a sharp smack round the head. *Serve him right,* immediately thought Jack. But then he felt rather shocked, his father had often been impatient with him, but he would never smack him hard like that. Momentarily he felt sorry for Nick.

'Are you OK Twiggy?' asked Henry kindly. 'If you are not, we can go down in the lift and join your parents and Marine. I'm sure that would be sensible.'

Twiggy blew her nose and took a couple of deep breaths, she liked to see herself as tough and independent and the wine was taking the edge off the pain, so she shook her head and put her snow goggles on, even though it hurt her face. At least it stopped Henry from seeing the real damage. Her face hurt a lot.
'I'm fine. Come on everybody let's run and beat them!' Catching everyone unawares, she gathered her sledge and ran towards the start.

'Wait for me!' shouted Blue.

'I'm coming!' roared Jack.

'Hang on!' called out Henry.

And this is how they arrived at the start of a long and occasionally steep toboggan run - at full speed, throwing themselves onto their sledges.

By the time they hit the second corner they were all out of control and travelling fast.

There was one piece of advice that Marine who had done the sledging before had given them. 'Whatever you do. Don't forget to wear your ski goggles.'

This was vital advice but Blue had forgotten it. The minute that Twiggy had rushed off, Blue had tripped over her sledge's rope and fallen flat on her face. In her effort to catch everybody up she had left her goggles round her neck. Now every time she braked wet snow flew into her face and eyes. Two glasses of hot wine had warmed her up and she felt that nothing mattered.

Recklessly she giggled to herself, 'Oh well. Easy decision… I just won't brake!'

She hit the third corner sideways yelling. At the last moment she pulled the right brake and straightened. She was impressed with herself when she discovered that pulling on the right corrected her slide. But now she picked up more speed and then she hurtled down the next straight, screaming even louder, if that was possible.

Jack, wearing his goggles, had made the corner as fast as he dared. He had started before Blue and was stunned to see her flying past going far faster that he could imagine himself going. She looked so out of control that all he could do was laugh with delighted horror. He shared the thrill of the speed, but the horrible anticipation of inevitable disaster, that Blue seemed headed for. Once he had heard someone say, 'She's an accident waiting for a place to happen.' Seeing Blue hurtling past, he suddenly understood the saying completely.

Despite Twiggy's flying start, Blue was catching up fast. She shot past two people who had fallen off their sledge, missing them by inches. Jack carefully negotiated round the fallers, hearing them call to each other, 'Did you see that girl? She's dangerous!'

'I hope she's going to be all right' said Jack to himself. He threw caution to the wind and he himself picked up some speed. If he applied the brakes lightly, he found that he could control the sledge.

There was another straight quite steep bit and then, just when everyone had picked up too much speed, the toboggan run turned into a well-known chicane. At least it was well known to the locals who gathered there to watch the fun!

But none of Nick's or Jack's party knew they were speeding into a very sharp couple of bends.

Nick was the first to arrive He was a big boy and his brute strength did not come with balance. His sledge skewed sideways and threw him off right in the middle of the slope. For a second Nick just sat there catching his breath. To rest was a mistake and a split second later the crowd gasped as they saw Blue hurtling round the corner. She had nowhere to go and anyway, even if there had been an escape route, she was semi blind from the snow and completely out of control.

Only a breath beat before, she had passed Twiggy who, like Jack, had gasped at the speed Blue was travelling. Twiggy's sixth sense told her to slow down before the blind bend. This was a wise move, as she had shed off a whole lot of speed when she came round the corner to witness Blue, flying in the air straight for the supine Nick.

She saw Blue hit Nick broadside on, their bodies collided and in mid-air Blue's elbow buried into Nick's face. A second later and Twiggy too was coming off her sledge and reluctantly using

Nick as a soft bolster to cushion her fall, ending up next to Blue. The next few other sledgers came round the corner to add their bodies to the general melee. It was chaos. But as quickly as they came off their sledges, the people jumped up knowing that there were others behind them and pulled their sledges to one side, which is how, when Jack arrived, he managed somehow to miss them all. He steered round the heap of bodies and sledges … and out the other side.

As he passed by, he looked in astonishment at the sight that met his eyes.

Nick was yelling, 'I'm hurt, I'm hurt! Get an ambulance!'

Blue and Twiggy had their arms round each other and seemed to be sobbing with laughter.

Other people on the run were picking themselves off the snow; there was a babel of different languages as people called out in surprise or concern mixed with laughter. Others were yelling, 'Slow down!' to the people coming round the blind bend, to no avail.

There was no help that Jack could give, he was already whizzing along a comparatively empty run.

'Wowee!' he cried, as he saw the finishing line ahead. There was Marine and Nick's mother. Mark was there too waving a handkerchief and hopefully, thought Jack … ten pounds!

'Jack, go Jack, go!' called Marine. Jack slid over the finishing line with a grin on his face.

'That was fantastic fun!'

'Where's Nicky?' asked Nick's mother looking up the slope.

''Ow come you are so far ahead Jack?' laughed Marine.

'Well, there was a bit of an accident on a corner,' started Jack and he told her all about it.

'Poor Nicky. Is he hurt?' gasped Nick's mother.

'Well, his lungs certainly aren't!' replied Jack.

Then a movement caught his eye and he saw that Blue and Twiggy were finishing and cheering each other loudly. Further behind them he could see Nick making his way cautiously down the slope. *Bother,* thought Jack.
Blue approached Marine looking rather uncomfortable, but at the same time pleased with herself.

'Where is 'Enri?' asked Marine.

'Dad is just behind, look he is coming now.'

They all cheered Henry across the line. He looked as though he had applied the brakes *all* the way down, he was covered with snow.

'Phew! That was terrifyingly uncomfortable and is the first and last time I do that,' he laughed. 'The young went off like mad things, then I found them all in a heap round the next corner, I'm not surprised they were going so fast, and that other boy, yelling for an ambulance, with nothing wrong with him at all. What a ridiculous fuss!' he stopped suddenly realising that Nick's mother was standing right by him.

'Time to go back to the hotel I think,' he said quickly and meaningfully to Marine.

Once they were all in the car, Henry turned to Blue.

'I say, darling, you were going like a bat out of hell. Was it you who hit Nick?'

'It wasn't my fault,' said Blue. 'I couldn't see and he was sprawled all over the corner. I just had to go into him, but there was a terrible whump when I hit him,' and she burst out laughing.

'Ambulance! Ambulance!' cried Twiggy and in moments the car was full of the sound of laughter, including Marine who was not quite sure what the joke was about.

'You may laugh, but it will be me who has to deal with his father,' said Henry soberly. 'I just know he will have something to say tomorrow at breakfast.'

Chapter 6

The next morning there was no Marine. She had taken a lift with someone to Chambery to fly home. First down for breakfast was Jack followed by Henry.

'Ahh, this is what I like: a boy's breakfast without those chattering women.' Henry said jovially. His smile darkened as he saw Nick and Nick's father approaching.

'I would just like you to see what your daughter's irresponsible action has caused my son,' Nick's father pontificated. He pushed Nick forward. Nick's right eye had some bruising and it was half closed.

Henry stood up concerned. 'Oh dear, well here she comes now and I'm sure she will apologise.'

Twiggy was leading Blue. As Twiggy approached it was clear to see that she had a cut under her eye and her eye was rather more bruised and colourful than Nick's.

'Good heavens! Twiggy, how did that happen?' asked Henry.

'It was the snowball that he threw at me: it wasn't snow at all it was a lump of ice,' accused Twiggy.

There was a small pause as Nick and his father looked uncomfortable.

'Fifteen all I think,' announced Henry determinedly, 'And if you don't mind I think we must get on and eat our breakfasts or we will never get to ski school.' With that he sat down and asked Jack to pass the confiture.

Nick and his father realised there was nothing they could do, other than moving to their table, which was Jack noticed thankfully, on the other side of the restaurant.

'Does it hurt?' asked Jack.

'It doesn't now, but it hurt awfully last night,' said Twiggy bravely. 'I had better go and join Mum and Dad. I bet they try and stop me skiing to today, but I'm not going to let them.'

There was a bit of a scramble to get to ski school that day. Somebody had moved Jack's board again; it never seemed to be where he left it. Every morning it was either by the window or the door as if it wanted to get out.

It seemed pleased to see him, starting up its little hum the moment he stepped outside on the snow, or was it the wind in the trees? Henry had elected to escort Twiggy to the ski school as well as his two children and Twiggy explained that she had promised to stop at lunchtime if her eye was hurting. There was no sign of Nick or his parents.

Much to Jack's surprise his snowboarding instructor had asked that he be moved into a higher class. This meant that he had to make friends all over again, but the group he was with were much closer in age and they were perfectly friendly on the occasions when they went up a lift. There was not much time to chat on the slope as their teacher kept them moving. They boarded right over two valleys away. By the time it was lunch, Jack felt he had boarded several miles.

Twiggy and Blue felt that they had had a busy morning too, and it was a quieter group that sat down to lunch to eat their usual choice, a big plate of chips and a burger.

Twiggy and Blue were firm friends now, but Twiggy's parents wanted to ski with their daughter in the afternoon and they invited Blue too, leaving Henry and Jack together.

'Let's try some lower slopes in the trees. Look we can ski right down the valley to a place called Brides-Les-Bains,' Henry showed Jack the map. As they set off Jack was aware that his board was humming louder than ever.

'Dad, you must be able to hear it,' he pointed out as he passed his father effortlessly.

'Yes,' said his father, 'It does make a rather unusual noise. It must be the type of snow; perhaps it's icier here, or dryer.' Father and son boarded and skied down paths and slopes that were tree lined. At one stage they had to cross a road and then ski through a little village. Under one of the houses they heard a quiet moo of a cow which was living inside for the winter, waiting for spring, then she could be let out to eat the delicate grasses and wild flowers. This diet would make her milk uniquely delicious.

'Just hearing that cow makes me hungry for a Tarte au Beaufort,' said Henry.

'It makes me think of ice cream,' laughed Jack.

It was a magical ski. Towards the bottom the path narrowed and switchbacked its way through the trees. Henry yodelled when he felt that the bend was particularly sharp, and Jack yelled back when he had got round it safely. What a wonderful thing it was for father and son to share that experience.

At the bottom, perfectly placed, was a lift where there were few other skiers. It was a long journey to the top and Jack would rather have preferred it if his Dad had not asked him how he found Marine but he was able to answer, quite truthfully, that she seemed nice enough.

'Just nice enough?' asked Dad a little forlornly.

'Are you going to marry her?' blurted Jack surprising himself.

'Well, this is real men's talk,' answered Henry. 'Perhaps, but I'm not sure that Blue would approve or you, and I would obviously like your approval?'

'I'd be worried about Mum,' said Jack loyally.

'So would I,' replied his dad, 'I would have to ask your Mum for her blessing first.'

'If she was Ok about it, then I would be,' said Jack feeling most adult, but not sure that he really believed what he was saying.

'That seems fair,' acknowledged his father.

He was heartily relieved when the ski bubble pulled into the last station and they had to get out. But he *did* feel a small bubble of pride that he had handled the conversation in a mature fashion, although he could not imagine how Blue would feel.

Blue and Twiggy were only quite envious of the long ski run that Jack and his father had done and they were bursting to share their own story. They too had had a fantastic time; Twiggy's parents had decided not to ski after all, so the girls had been allowed to ski on the home run themselves. They had met several parties of people their age doing the same.

'There's a wonderful switchback track which goes through the woods and just when you've got far too much speed it gets really narrow and you can't brake, and then it spits you out onto the slope at high speed!' gabbled Twiggy. 'It's like being on Nemesis!'

Jack was grateful that he had been on Nemesis so he did not have to ask what it was. It gave him a warm glow to be with the girls, especially Twiggy who talked to him as though he was the only person there. He felt included in a way he had never been before. *Girls aren't too bad at all,* he thought to himself.

He noticed that his father had been on his mobile talking animatedly for some time. Henry came over, looking worried.

'I'm sorry to have to say that we are going to have to go home guys. Marine has met all sorts of problems and needs my help. It's really bad luck but I think we'll have to go first thing tomorrow.'

Jack and Blue looked aghast at the awful news but Twiggy got up quickly and went to meet her parents who were coming into the reception area. There was a quick conversation and Twiggy's parents, Mark and Lucy came over.

'Henry, we are absolutely serious, we would be delighted to act in loco parentis for Blue and Jack. It all works perfectly as we are travelling on the same plane back. They are all getting on so well… We can look after them, if that would make them happy.'

'Yes please!' exclaimed Jack and Blue together.

'What, both of them?' said Dad. 'Perhaps I should take Jack back then you'll only have one.' Jack's face said it all. He looked at his father horrified. Mark laughed.

'I would be particularly disappointed to lose Jack. Far too many women in one party; we men have got to stick together.'

'Please Dad,' begged Blue.

'I will have to ring your mother to get her agreement. It is incredibly kind of you to offer.' Henry went discreetly away and when he had spoken to Jack and Blue's mother he said that they should talk to her too. By the time Jack and Blue had spoken to her, she did not need any more convincing. It was decided that Jack and Blue would stay on.

'Perhaps you should stick together, and we will take you out of ski school,' said Mark.

This was an even better idea, 'We can show you our way through the woods,' said Twiggy to Jack.

Apart from Henry who was very sorry to be leaving, the rest of the party went to bed with high spirits. But just before he went to his room, Jack went along to the ski locker room to see if he could catch who was moving his board every night.

His board was exactly where he had left it, but he was sure that he could hear it humming. The board seemed to be reflecting Jack's mood, excited anticipation about tomorrow. To make perfectly sure that it was his board making the noise. Jack moved around the ski locker so he could listen from every angle. No, there was only one place the hum was coming from, and that was his board. He went dashing upstairs to get the girls and prove once and for all that his board sang on its own. Rounding the corner, he cannoned into Nick.

Despite Jack's horrified apology, Nick swore dramatically and swung a fist at Jack, followed by a well-aimed kick. Nick was comfortably bigger than Jack and the fist glanced over the top of his shoulder but the kick caught him on the leg and hurt.

'You're a nasty bully,' accused Jack to the departing Nick. Nick threatened to come upstairs again after him but Jack was nimble and disappeared as Nick yelled after him, 'Loser!'

Why, oh why does he have to be in the same hotel? thought Jack for the hundredth time.

He was determined not to let the girls know that he had come off worse with Nick. He knocked on their door and they let him in. He considered suggesting that they come down to the ski locker room to listen to his board but something stopped him. Just suppose it was not making a noise and that Nick got to hear that Jack had a board that sang to him! He would never live that one down. He went a bit quiet and Blue thought he might be missing their Dad, so she went to extra lengths to try and cheer him up.

It was sometime later that he left the girls' room and made his way down the hotel stairs to his room. As he put his card into his room he heard his hotel telephone ringing. What a dilemma. It could be his father or the girls - or Nick. Nervously Jack picked up the receiver. To his relief it was Blue and Twiggy, who were giggling and blowing kisses down the receiver.

Honestly girls! thought Jack, but he went to sleep in a much more cheerful frame of mind.

Chapter 7

The next morning had an altogether different aspect. Pierre told them it was a lot warmer and this had created foggy areas; one moment you could not see out of the hotel window and the next you could see right to the sky.

'That'll make it even more fun!' exclaimed Twiggy enthusiastically. Jack was not sure, he preferred to be able to see all the time. But he felt that whatever the visibility, the day would be completely wonderful. Here he was totally wrong.

The first massive disappointment was when Twiggy's father arrived and sat down at the table.

'I've been asked by Mrs Mandelson, whether you wouldn't mind skiing with her son today; Mr Mandelson was very ill last night and Mrs Mandelson has had to go to hospital with him. She rang me very early this morning and I promised we would look after him.'

'Mrs Mandelson?' questioned Blue. But Jack did not need to ask. He knew the Mandelson's boy… it was the bully Nick.

'Do we have to Dad?' asked Twiggy earnestly.

'Now Twiggy, I know you don't like him but this is just one of those things. Just for one day I'm asking you to help out. Please don't make it an issue,' said Mark, her father.

'He could go to ski school for the day,' insisted Twiggy.

'That is not what is going to happen. His Mother says he's hating ski school and I felt I had to help her out. As far as I can gather, Nick's father could be seriously ill and imagine if we were in the same position?'

It seemed that Nick could not stay with Twiggy's mother either as she was driving Henry to the airport.

Twiggy, Blue and Jack were silent. They could see there was no way out.

'If Mr Mandelson doesn't get better, will Nick have to come with us every day?' asked Jack in a small voice.

'Oh come on Jack, he can't be that bad!' exclaimed Mark exasperated. 'No, as I understand it, they are trying to organise an air ambulance to get him home, and in that case obviously Nick and his mother will go too. He can stay with Lucy this afternoon, she should be back by three.'

Jack willed the air ambulance to wing its way to the door of the hospital as quickly as possible, or probably the roof of the hospital, he thought, remembering a film he had seen.

The rest of breakfast became a silent affair.

'Nick will meet you at the bottom of the ski lift at exactly nine o'clock. I am relying on you all to be ready and there at that time. Don't let me down guys,' warned Mark.

'We'll just have to do it, and somehow get through the day,' said Blue sighing.

Just before nine the three traipsed out with Twiggy's father to the ski lift. Waiting at the bottom was Nick. He scowled at them.

'We're so sorry to hear about your father,' started Mark as Nick looked at the ground. 'Now, you are all to stick together. If one of you gets hurt, this is what is to happen: one person must stay with the person who is hurt, the others must look for a grown up, preferably a ski teacher, you know how to recognise them and there are always lots of ski instructors teaching beginners on this run, that is the only time that you split up. Can I have a 'yes' from each of you to show me that you understand?'

Each of them told Twiggy's father that they understood.

'Nick, your mother said that she had given you some money for a mid-morning hot chocolate for everyone. That is very kind and you can come back to the hotel for a late lunch. I should be finished by then.'

They nodded, although Jack thought his chances of getting a hot chocolate from Nick were practically nil.

'One last thing,' said Mark, 'can I see that you all have your mobiles in your hand right now, so that we can swap numbers and then I can check you're all right through the day.'

Everyone got out their mobiles except Jack.

Nick held out his. Blue looked at it and gasped.

'That's Jack's,' she accused Nick. 'It's got that sticker I gave him!'

'It's mine' replied Nick stubbornly.

Mark looked on confused.

'Where's yours Jack?' he asked. Jack made a hopeless gesture towards Nick's mobile. Nick glowered at him.

'It was stolen from me at school,' he glowered back at Nick.

'Oh dear I just don't have time for this,' said Mark exasperatedly. 'I have an important conference call in only five minutes. Look you lot, you are just going to have to get on for today. We'll talk later on this morning, and I will come and join you. Whatever you do, Jack you must not get separated from the others. If you do, ski back here and stay in the hotel and the others will find you there, is that clear?'

They had to agree to the plan. Mark marched off leaving them together uncomfortably in a group at the bottom of the ski lift. There was a pause and then Blue took control.

'Come on, let's go for a run and see what it's like,' she said determinedly.

By dint of edging and squirming through the thin queue, and sending each other meaningful glances, Blue, Twiggy and Jack managed to get onto the ski lift by themselves, without Nick.

'Hooray, a Nick-free zone,' announced Twiggy as they swung through the air. 'Dad did not say we had to take lifts together,' she added defensively.

For a second Jack felt almost sorry for Nick sitting on a lift behind, all by himself. Then he remembered that in Nick's pocket was his - Jack's - mobile, a present from his father, and he felt righteously angry.

The morning did not go well, for a start Nick did not seem to be able to ski very well, he fell over a lot at the top where it was a bit steeper. He kept on whining about his bindings being loose.

'Faker!' Twiggy hissed.

Sometimes a mist would appear from nowhere and then all of them had to creep along. It was surprisingly difficult to read the slope when the visibility went. There was a moment when Nick with a hint of contrition in his voice offered them all a hot chocolate.

'No. We prefer to keep skiing,' answered Blue primly, although with the fog it would have been infinitely preferable to sit inside with a hot chocolate. When Nick pointed this out, Blue countered, 'Three against one,' and there was no answer to that one.

They skied on only to stop again to wait for Nick. Suddenly out of the gloom appeared Pierre boarding at speed. He skidded to a stop sending a shower of snow over Blue who squealed 'Pierre, you're such a good boarder!' They had a chat and Pierre seemed to think he could help Nick; he adjusted his bindings slightly.

'I recommend the run right down the valley, it is through the trees and the visibility is always better,' pointed out Pierre. 'It is not at all steep, it is vairy easy.'

'Can you show us?' asked Blue. But Pierre had to get back to the hotel to help in the kitchen.

'I know the way, I did it yesterday with Dad,' said Jack.

'It would be really good fun to do a new run; I'm bored with this one,' enthused Twiggy.

'Yes, but will Nick manage it?' asked Blue within Nick's hearing.

'Of course I will now my bindings sorted out. You try and ski with loose bindings,' retorted Nick. 'It seems to me that the real question is, does your *little* brother really know the way? That's what we should be worrying about.'

'Course Jack knows the way,' said Blue, 'don't you Jack?'

'Course I do,' said Jack promptly whilst he desperately tried to remind himself of the way. His board gave a sudden hum and he felt more confident. He looked up to find the rest of the party looking at him. He realised that they were waiting for him to be the leader. Before his courage evaporated he called, 'Follow me!' and he boarded away below the hotel and down towards the woods.

Chapter 8

The first part of the run was relatively open. Few people had skied it and apart from Jack everyone had falls in the deep snow. There was one place where Blue hit something under the snow… her skis came to an abrupt stop, but not Blue, she sailed on in a graceful arc through the air as if she was diving and landed upside down, completely unhurt. Their laughter rang through the clear air and even Nick managed a wan smile. But poor Nick was struggling. His face was red and sweaty, he had removed various bits of clothing, his goggles hung round his neck, his hat peeped out from his pocket. And his gloves? Well his gloves were nowhere to be seen.

'What's that?' asked Twiggy.

'What?' asked Blue?

'Is that smoke?' asked Twiggy.

They looked to where she was pointing: a wind was flowing up the mountain being pushed or pulled by a huge bank of fog. They looked at the billowing mass with fascination until it started to blot out the sun and suddenly the day became grey.

'We need to get to the woods,' called Jack 'Quickly. Then we will have some visibility.'

The slight panic in his voice galvanised them into sudden movement and Blue promptly fell.

'Wait!' she called.

They all stopped except for Nick who was making for the safety of the trees.

Blue got up quickly and they set off, the fog enveloped them and it was almost impossible to see the edge of the wood, it appeared only as a deeper grey in front of them.

'Nick!' they yelled, but there was no answer.

'We can follow his tracks,' said Twiggy. Edging slowly along they followed Nick's wide and erratic trail over the snow.

'I'm sure this is the wrong direction,' said Jack crossly.

'Nick!' they all yelled. But still there was no reply.

'If he can't answer he deserves to be lost,' said Blue dismissively. 'He must be able to hear us.'

'Perhaps he fell and hurt himself?' suggested Jack as they came to stop for what seemed the hundredth time.

'If he's hurt himself we would hear a cry for an ambulance all over the mountain,' giggled Twiggy. This started the other two laughing. Feeling a little better they dropped steadily and slowly towards the wood. But even with their best attempts to keep in sight of each other, the fog was so deep there was a moment when Jack could see neither girl. He called out sharply after them.

Unlike Nick they both answered quickly and found each other with relief.

'I think we should all make the call of some sort of animal every time we turn, in that way we can keep a constant check,' suggested Twiggy.

'I'll be a wolf!' said Jack eagerly.

'I'll make monkey noises' said Twiggy.

'And I'll moo,' was Blue's offering.

Extraordinary noises pierced the muffled atmosphere. Their silly attempts to sound like animals made them laugh and relax. They were able to board and ski a little faster, gaining confidence as they neared the wood. They could feel its shape and Jack fancied that he could smell the resinous conifer trees.

In the meantime, Nick, whose anger had been mounting at his own inadequacy, had in fact got all the way to the edge of the trees, without falling. He was aware of the others calling him, but as he hated always being the last and the worst - especially as he was the eldest - he was determined not to break his concentration, so he ignored the calls.

'Let them try and catch up and see what it's like,' he said to himself truculently. He thought he could see a track in the woods, so he followed that, and as it meandered gently into the trees he realised how still and quiet it was. He felt a frisson of fear.

'I'm here!' he shouted into the gloom. But there was absolute silence.

'I'm here, right here!' he shouted again. He listened and then heard the blood-curdling howl of a wolf.

'Oh no, no, no!' gasped Nick. 'Help me anyone help, anyone help, help!' A small sob escaped his lips, he shivered and searched for his gloves, but he seemed to have lost them.

The wolf howled again, a monkey gibbered and a cow mooed a little further away. Then around the corner Jack appeared, his howl stopping half way as he saw Nick.

'He's here!' shouted Jack unnecessarily loudly as Twiggy and then Blue followed him round the second bend.

'Why didn't you answer?' asked Blue angrily.

'I didn't hear you,' said Nick miserably.

'You're such a liar,' dismissed Twiggy.

'Now where do we go?' asked Blue executing one of her neat little turns on the narrowing path.

'Is this the right way Jack?' asked Blue.

'I'm not sure it is, because I didn't see a sign when we came onto the track, and yesterday I saw lots of signs,' said Jack.

'Do you mean you've lost the way?' asked Nick accusingly.

This was so unfair that for a moment Jack was lost for words, and then he asked angrily, 'Who led us into the wrong path?'

Three sets of eyes looked at Nick. He looked away.

'This is the right direction,' said Jack, 'I'm sure of it. If we work our way along a little bit to the right, we should hit the path, but this time we really must stick together. I'll go first and Blue you bring up the rear and we'll see where we get to?' To his surprise everyone accepted this suggestion without demur, and he zigzagged his way through the trees which luckily at this part of the forest were not too tightly packed together.

After five more turns they had gone a lot lower and it seemed clearer in the sky above them. The only problem was that the sky did not seem so bright. *It must be well after lunch,* thought Jack as he realised how hungry he was. They stopped to catch their breath.

'Jack, I am going to have to ring Twiggy's Dad and tell him we are lost. It's half past one already, Mark will be expecting us for lunch,' said Blue.

'OK,' said Jack 'I'm sorry that we're lost.' He looked forlorn.

'Don't worry old chap,' said Blue sounding like his father, 'It's completely not your fault. I know everyone will be furious, but I don't know what else to do.'

She turned back to the others and told them she was going to phone Twiggy's father.

Twiggy looked miserable. 'Couldn't we look for the path a little longer, Dad will be so annoyed.'

'I'm starving,' said Nick. 'The sooner we get out of this wood the better.'

Blue had found her mobile, 'We'll have to use someone else's. I haven't got a signal.'

Twiggy found hers. 'Nor have I,' she said. They all looked at Nick. He looked dishevelled and instead of hot, he looked shivery. He started to look in all the pockets of his jacket and trousers. He looked once and then tried again, with increasing panic.

'Damn it! I've lost my hat, my gloves, my mobile *and* my money. I should never have come with you. I should have known it would be awful.'

'Don't think we wanted you to ski with us either!' retorted Twiggy loudly.

'If you hadn't led, we would be at the bottom of the run by now and coming back. A*nd* you keep falling!' accused Blue.

'That was my binding. After it was mended, I skied better than all of you,' countered Nick. At this both girls hurled insults at Nick whilst he shouted back. The vitriolic argument was interrupted by a loud anguished cry a little below them.

'What was that?' whispered Twiggy.

'That's the same cry that we heard at the airport,' hissed back Jack. 'Don't you remember Blue?' he asked.

'Give it up Jack, that's such a stupid thing to say,' said Blue rounding on him.

'But *it is,*' said Jack ignoring her, 'it's that creature we've seen before, I know it is,' and as he said that his board started to move of its own volition towards the noise.

'Jack stop, don't go that way. It might be a man-eating bear,' shrieked Twiggy.

But Jack could not stop his board.

'You must come with me!' he shouted back, 'I can't stop!' he cried, his voice getting quieter as he disappeared into the trees.

'Come on!' said Blue, stepping her skis round a half circle so she could follow Jack. Twiggy hesitated.

'I am absolutely not following that stupid boy straight into the jaws of a grizzly bear,' announced Nick. That made Twiggy's mind up.

'We've got no signal and no one knows where we are. I'm going and I couldn't care less whether you follow or not, and by the way, there aren't grizzly bears in the Alps, everyone knows that,' and Twiggy and Blue skied after Jack calling, 'Wait!'

'Sugar!' said Nick as he scrambled to his feet. *I hate you Twiggy, he thought to himself, and I hate you Blue and most of all I really hate Jack.* He muttered this miserable mantra to himself all down the slope and, somehow, he managed not to fall. He came out of the trees to find himself in a small snow field carved out of the forest, with Twiggy not far in front and Blue disappearing again into the trees on the far side. How far in front of Blue was Jack, he could not imagine. He was just relieved that the snow field was not steep and the conditions were perfect for skiing.

However, unbeknown to the foursome, the snow field was on the edge of a steep drop off. It was difficult to see because at the bottom of the field was another wood looking innocent enough with a clear track leading into it, but as Jack found to his cost, the very next bend dropped straight into a void. It was so steep, he had no chance to stop. He just fell through the air for what felt like ages, bounced once on a snow-covered rock and landed several feet below on a snowy ledge.

'Watch out!' he yelled, but too late … one by one they followed him. Twiggy landed on her bum once, but when she hit the next bump she was thrown into standing position again, and so much to her amazement she arrived next to Jack upright on her skiis.

'That was awesome,' said Jack with admiration.

Blue did not land so elegantly. She was thrown off course and came around the rock with a little scream. She skied under a branch which dumped its winter load of snow on top of her.

Nick yelled loudly from the top to the bottom of his fall, but he was so winded when he landed that he remained entirely silent for several seconds. When at last he caught his breath, his anger knew no bounds: he threw off his skiis, sank straight up to his thighs in the snow, whereupon he punched uselessly at the air round him and started sobbing loudly.

'I've had enough, I'm cold and I'm going to die here,' he sobbed.

'Don't be ridiculous!' retorted Blue. But in truth she was worried, she was cold too and she could see the daylight going. She also knew that to keep someone warm you should hug them to you, *but not Nick,* she thought guiltily, *he can freeze for all I care.* She checked her mobile again, there was still no signal.

'What are we going to do?' asked Twiggy.

'I think we are getting into worse and worse trouble, we need to find shelter and then wait for someone to find us,' suggested Blue.

'But no one knows where we are,' said Twiggy.

'Pierre will remember that he recommended this run to us,' said Blue suddenly. 'He'll tell someone and Mark will have tried to ring us by now. Everyone will realise that something's not right.'

'I'll look for some shelter,' said Jack. In truth his board seemed to want to slip further down. *I'm sure it's trying to go by itself, it's not me,* thought Jack.

'Don't go far. Are you ready Nick? You've just got to make one more effort,' encouraged Blue, her voice softening as she recognised how miserable Nick really was.

'Look, I've got a spare pair of gloves,' said Twiggy kindly. 'They're inner gloves, so they aren't waterproof, but better than nothing.'

Nick took them without a word of thanks. Blue and Twiggy exchanged despairing looks.

Jack had edged on a little way, 'I've found a cave! Come on, it's out of the wind.' He had no sooner finished calling when the great haunting cry came again, followed by a terrible howling. Jack had pretended to be a wolf but this noise was completely different. This was the noise that you would imagine a pack of massive wolves would make if they were hunting something that they were about to catch, full of hysterical yipping and excited shrieking - and it was coming in their direction. The noise grew louder and louder and just above them they heard something brushing through the undergrowth. The girls screamed, Nick scrambled to his legs clutching his skis, he half swam and waded through the snow after the girls who followed Jack down, round the corner and into a cave.

'They're after us!' gasped Twiggy.
'Keep quiet!' hissed Blue, 'and they won't find us.'

They kept silent except for one noise – a loud and insistent hum. It was Jack's board. They all looked at the board aghast.

'How's it making that noise?' demanded Blue.

'Shut it up Jack!' hissed Twiggy.

'I don't know how to,' replied Jack desperately.

Suddenly the cave went black. The girls screamed and the boys yelled with shock. Blocking the light and standing in the entrance was a large hooded figure.

Chapter 9

The hooded figure moved into the cave. Twiggy gave a little whimper and Nick pressed himself into a corner and buried his head into his jacket. Blue scrambled backwards.

Above them they could hear the wolf noises pause briefly and then gather strength.

Only Jack held his ground, standing and staring at the figure.

The figure looked at Jack and spoke to him in a deep rumble.

'Jack you must place your board in the entrance and stand firm with me, it is time.'

'Time for what?' whispered Twiggy to herself. She could hear her teeth chattering with fear.

For a moment Jack was taken back to the attic. He remembered the warm feel of the little bear man as he pressed him to the bottom of his pocket. He remembered how it was so much bigger in his backpack, and now here was the identical figure, alive and huge in front of him! He could do nothing but obey the figure's command and so he marched to the entrance of the cave. With all the courage he could muster he held his board upright, its base facing the outside. The figure stood next to him.

'Now what?' Jack tried to shout above the noise of the oncoming howling pack, but all that came out of his mouth was an anguished shriek.

Twiggy never heard the answer, for all at once the wolves arrived at the entrance. The noise was awful. Their breath stunk of rotting flesh and it filled the cave making her stomach turn over. Next to her Nick groaned and vomited uninhibitedly.

'It's all over, we're finished!' he gasped.

'Not without a fight!' muttered Blue. Nick's wail was the impetus she needed to regain her courage. She could see her little brother confronting the wolves, she could see their teeth and the whites of their eyes.

'I'm coming Jack!' she yelled and charged through the cave carrying one of her skis like a weapon.

The figure put out a leathery and hairy hand to stop her hurling herself on the wolves.

'Place your hand and your courage on Jack's board,' he commanded. He picked up Blue's trembling hand and placed in on the board.

All three of them held the snowboard. Its hum went from a loud and insistent noise to a higher and higher note. As the note got higher, Twiggy gritted her teeth. Nick pressed his hands to his ears and curled into a tight ball. The sound was so horrible to hear that, when the figure took one hairy hand and pressed Blue's head against his body shielding her ears, she did not complain. He did the same to Jack, leaving Blue and Jack holding onto the screaming board and the nearest wolves flinched and turned away. Still the board's notes got higher until the frequency was so high that Jack and Blue could no longer hear it…but the wolves could. One by one they turned their heads whimpering and eventually they loped off into the darkness, until none were left.

There was a silence in the cave until Twiggy asked in a small voice, 'Have they gone?'

'They have gone, but not far. They will attack again, they do not give up easily,' replied the figure. He turned to Jack, 'You have found the entrance only just in time.'

'Well, I wasn't really looking for it. It just appeared,' said Jack awkwardly.

'We must make our way into the mountains where the wolves cannot follow. Come,' ordered the figure.

'Where?' asked Twiggy and then more shyly, 'What's your name?'

The figure looked down at her for a moment. 'Where we go will depend on The Fault lines, as for my name, you may call me Theta. We can talk when we are safe; for now we must go quickly. Follow me,' he ordered.

Blue, Twiggy and Jack came to Theta's side. Nick looked at them in amazement.

'If you think I am going with that, in there,' he started pointing at the dark tunnel, 'you must be off your heads.'

'If you stay you will make a good meal for the wolves,' nodded Theta looking closely at Nick. In the failing light he could see how frightened they all were. 'Wait, I will make light,' he concentrated on his huge hands and eventually a green glow appeared. It lit the ground in front of them and spread an eerie light upon their faces.

'It is enough; we leave,' he started down the tunnel. Outside and not far away they heard a faint howl, it was answered by another cry, but this one was much closer.

Nick stood up quickly, 'I'm coming too, wait for me,' he said and lumbered down the tunnel after them.

'They're coming,' whimpered Twiggy as one howl was joined by several more yips.

Theta turned to Blue, 'You have shown courage. The wolves will be cautious of you. You will go last and protect us.'

Blue's eyes looked huge in the low light of the green glow coming from between Theta's hands.

'I'm not sure that I can; I'm frightened,' she whispered to Theta.

Theta bent down towards her. He said something quietly to Blue which the others could not hear, all they heard was a faint rumbling, a sound like a distant avalanche, but they saw Blue nodding and standing straighter. She put her skis on her shoulder and her poles in her hand.

'There's no point taking those,' said Nick.

'On the contrary,' replied Theta, 'where we are going you cannot follow unless you have your bearers.'

Nick sighed theatrically, he lifted his skis under his arm.

'You will take Blue's poles,' commanded Theta.

'I won't,' disagreed Nick automatically. But even as he was speaking the poles were flying from Blue to Nick. Nick tried to chuck them away, but they were stuck to his hand.

'OK then,' he agreed gracelessly.

There was a cautious pattering noise behind them … the wolves were entering the cave.

As Theta moved ahead swiftly, the others hustled round him, loathe to be left behind to face the wolves without light.

They came to the back of the cave where Theta pushed aside a boulder which, although half his size, was still a tremendous weight.

As he was closing the boulder the leading wolf appeared. It moved cautiously, its body low to the ground.

'It's so huge!' Twiggy gasped.
The wolf could see that the boulder was going to roll back into position before he and his pack could get through. Instead of leaping at the narrowing gap, he did the most peculiar thing, he

rolled onto his back. A smell of damp carpets pervaded the already musty air.

'Close the gap,' urged Jack.

But instead Theta said to the wolf, 'I see you.'

The wolf then yipped back to Theta.

'It's as if he is talking to him,' whispered Blue, her fascination briefly overcoming her terror.

'He is,' whispered back Twiggy. 'He's asking for a favour, he wants to come through with the rest of the pack.'

'No way,' shuddered Nick who was hiding behind the boulder 'Even if you did understand what they are saying which you don't.'

'He's saying he wants to come home too, with Theta, he's saying that he does not want to be cut off in this world where there are too many men,' went on Twiggy whispering so that Theta could not hear.

'And Theta is saying that if they come through, they will prey on *his* people, and men will come through this gap, and despoil the lands.'

The wolf answered back in little barks and yips.
'What's he saying Twiggy?' asked Blue and Jack together, not questioning whether Twiggy could understand the interaction that was clearly going on between Theta and the wolf.

'He's saying that he will impose the law of the pack, that he will ensure our safety if Theta leaves a gap and does not roll the boulder across, and that he will leave one wolf always as sentry to stand guard over the tunnel. He is saying that the sentry will guard the tunnel with his life,' translated Twiggy quietly to them.

Theta lowered his voice and spoke only to the leader of the wolf pack, 'Quiviuk, I trust you, but you are old, there are others who seek to take your place, I can see this by the scars in your fur, they are not just hunting scars, but the scars of your own kind. How can I be confident that all your pack will keep their word?' At this the wolf that was no longer grovelling on his back but sitting on his haunches, stood up. He slinked a little closer to Theta. Theta responded by closing the boulder a little more. Behind, the other wolves started growling and muttering, angered as they saw their escape route closing.

'Wait!' called the great wolf. 'I speak to the pack.'

'What's happening?' asked Blue.

'He's asking every member of the pack to swear individually to Theta that he will keep his word,' replied Twiggy in her normal voice. Theta's attention was broken from the wolves and he glanced down at Twiggy curiously.

'How do you speak wolf?' he asked gently.

As Twiggy realised that she was the only one, apart from Theta who could understand what the wolves were saying, wonderment came over her face 'I've absolutely no idea, I just can,' she whispered blushing.

In the meantime, one wolf after another pushed past the leader and spoke shortly to Theta. Most of them did it quickly without looking at Theta, but three stared at him boldly and made their oath proudly. One of those three clearly intended to be the next leader of this pack.

'I've seen wolves in the wild before,' whispered Twiggy to Theta, 'but these wolves are much bigger, is it because they are so close?'

'No,' said Theta. 'This is the Ravening Wolf family; they are twice the size of the wolves that your world knows. They are craftier and I hate to put my trust in them, but I have become weak in your world. It won't be long before they realise that they are strong enough to push the boulder enough to squeeze through and I cannot protect you for ever, so it is best to make a contract with them now, to give us time to escape from them. I do not know how long they will be able to keep their word. They are hungry, even now they are assessing my strength and what you would be like to eat.'

'Then we simply have no hope,' said Twiggy faintly, hoping that the others had not heard.

'We do. They know that I am the only one who can lead them out of here,' replied Theta gravely. 'Do not let them know that you can understand their speech,' he went on, 'luckily they do not understand yours nor, when I speak to you, do they understand me.'

'But I understood you when you spoke to them,' said Twiggy.

'That's because I was using two-fold speech. It seems you understand two-fold speech too.'

Twiggy looked doubtful and blushed.

'It is time to move. You shall keep a meadow's distance,' he ordered the wolves. They shifted and squirmed. They were eager to move quickly and knew instinctively that their travelling would be much slower with the boys and girls.

For what seemed like hours they marched through the tunnel. The light from Theta threw their shadows onto the ceiling of the tunnel. The way was extraordinarily smooth, until suddenly they would have to skirt round a large boulder.

'This tunnel has been carved by melt water,' Theta told them.

Occasionally Blue's skis would catch the ceiling and there would be a clatter, but otherwise it was a silent and subdued party that trudged their way over the smooth rock. The wolves were incredibly quiet, Blue could not tell whether they were directly behind or keeping the required 'meadow's length'. Once when she had turned around she could see nothing but black, on another occasion she was able to see at least eight pairs of eyes glinting redly in Theta's light.

Eventually Twiggy said weakly, 'Can't we stop and rest?' and then she fainted straight onto the ground.

Theta picked her up gently and put her over his shoulder. 'I forget how weak men are, without your weapons you are nothing, I shall carry her.'

Nick spoke up, 'I'm shattered too and I haven't eaten since breakfast. We can't go on.'

Theta paused, 'I will take a path to water and we can rest there.'

'Why are we stopping?' yipped a wolf from close behind, making Blue jump.

'These youngsters are exhausted and must rest and water,' answered Theta.

Blue could feel the dissatisfaction running through the pack behind her.

Theta found a pool down a smaller tunnel leading off the main tunnel. Here they drank the pure water gratefully, high above they could see a hole in the ceiling and one bright star shone through. Twiggy regained consciousness and sipped the water. Her face looked unnaturally pale caught in Theta's green light.

I wish we were out there, thought Jack to himself as he looked at the star. He lay down but the ground was so hard that he thought he would never be able to rest. But what seemed like a too short time later, he was being woken by Theta and told to get up.
Although Twiggy was feeling better Theta said it would be wise if she was carried over his shoulder.

It was not long before Nick was clamouring to stop again and although Blue and Jack had not complained, they knew that they were exhausted too.

'We cannot stop again,' remonstrated Quiviuk the leader of the pack, as Theta put Twiggy down.

'They cannot go on,' responded Theta gravely.

There was a discussion amongst the wolves and Theta tensed, anticipating a bad outcome.

Quiviuk came forward, 'The female slave wolves will carry them.'

There was a pause whilst Theta considered this. Then he spoke to the children. 'I have seen that there are some she-wolves in the pack which is unusual. When the Ravening Wolves go hunting, usually they just take the males. But they have obviously stolen some females from another pack and they are ordering those females to carry you. I think we have no choice but to agree. If you do not ride a wolf, then the wolves will force me to leave you behind.'

The children considered this; one moment they were running from a terrifying pack of hungry animals and the next they were being told that they had to sit on the back of them.

'Won't they mind?' asked Twiggy.
'Oh, *very* much,' answered Theta, 'it will be the greatest indignity for them, but they will have to accept or be killed.'

'They have no choice and we have no choice,' said Blue soberly.

Four wolves were pushed forwards, they looked battle scarred and angry, but also subservient. One by one the children were placed on the backs of the female wolves. The four she-wolves stared into the middle distance as if to remove themselves from what was happening to them.

'They stink,' said Nick disgustedly.

'Shut up!' hissed Twiggy. 'We are lucky that they are tolerating us at all.'

She scratched the wolf behind its ear, just at the place where her dog liked a bit of a scratch. She felt the wolf lose a bit of tension under her. They moved off and there was immediately a commotion - Nick had fallen off, and without thinking the wolf had nipped him, as it might one of her cubs, for being so stupid.

Theta ignored Nick's moans and shoved him unceremoniously back onto the wolf showing him how to bury himself in its great pelt and hold onto its fur.

'Fall off again Nick and I'm very afraid that we must leave you,' said Theta and he turned and started to shuffle run down the tunnel.

The wolves leapt after him. The children clung on and there began a terrifying journey into the black hole.

Chapter 10

When it was completely dark all the children had to do was cling on tightly. Especially as they seemed to be travelling always up. Every so often a shaft of nightlight lit up the tunnel, then they could see how fast - frighteningly fast - they were travelling. If they fell off they would surely break a bone - or worse.

At last they came to a halt. In front was a great chasm in the rocks. Above the chasm, the rocks reached sheer to the sky. A huge moon tinged with pink sat impassively above them. Two wolves began to howl at it, their breath spiralling into the frosty night air.

Quiviuk looked at Theta and Theta back at Quiviuk.

'We must go over the gap?' asked Quiviuk of Theta.

'We must,' answered Theta shortly.

The gap stretched dark in front of them.

'Only the strongest of my pack can make this leap. I fear for myself and the older wolves. If it was only a stride shorter we might succeed.' He shook his great head. 'The she-slaves are excellent athletes, they are lithe and can jump far, but with a weight on their backs...' he broke off to reassess the gap again. 'Now is the time to leave the human cubs behind,' he announced.

'We must bring them with us,' said Theta. 'Only one of them can ride the board and so it is only he who can bring down the Great Avalanche that is threatening Valley Songinvelo. The Life Spirit is calling him…'

Twiggy listened to Theta talking and wondered who was the 'one'. Theta had said 'he'. *Surely it can't be Jack?* she thought with a shiver. *And who or what was the 'Life Spirit' who was calling him?* She looked back at the black gap in front of her, she imagined falling into it. She shivered and looked away.

The wolf under her shifted and spoke up, with a ringing voice she said, 'I will try to make this leap with the she-cub on my back, but if I succeed, I want my freedom.'

Twiggy scratched her behind the ear again supportively.

Theta looked at Quiviuk, 'We are running out of time, you must agree to the she-wolf's request.'

Quiviuk nodded, 'She won't make it though,' he snarled under his breath, but not so quietly that Twiggy could not hear.

'What's happening?' asked Blue nervously.

Theta glanced at Twiggy to stop her from answering in case she gave herself away, within Quiviuk's hearing. He answered Blue. 'The slave she-wolf is going to take Twiggy across.'

'What?' asked Nick aghast slipping off his wolf to stand on the ground. 'How? Nothing could get across that. Actually, it doesn't matter what happens anymore: I refuse to believe this is real. It's a nightmare and I'm just going to wake up and all you foul people are going to disappear.' A large tear ran down his cheek. 'Wake up, wake up!' he moaned to himself.

The she-wolf ran into the pack making room for a run up.

I'm so frightened, Twiggy thought to herself.

'Don't be frightened she-cub,' a voice answered back in her head 'I, Ilanna, can jump further than even the Ravening wolves can imagine. Just hold your head up and stare at the wall on the other side, this will keep your balance central above me, this will help me, can you do that?'

'Yes, I can,' said Twiggy in her head, wondering how she could communicate with the wolf without even speaking aloud. 'This must be a nightmare I am having,' she said to herself stoutly. 'There is nothing to be scared of, as I will wake up in a moment.'

Theta, Blue, Jack and Nick stood at the edge but to one side of the black abyss. Ilanna disappeared a little way back into the tunnel from where they had come from. There was a clattering of claws on the rock floor and something flew past the children, creating a rush of wind. It was Ilanna running and leaping. There was a moment of silence as the wolf flew through the air, then cheers of encouragement and yipping from the other she-wolves. Twiggy longed to screw her eyes tight shut but with a tremendous effort she kept them open, willing them both to arrive safely. It felt as though they were going to reach the other side easily, then Ilanna spoke in her head.

'Hold tight she-cub I'm going to give them something to think about!' The onlookers yelped and gasped as she dropped a back leg into the abyss. She had to scrabble hard to drag herself onto the other side.

'That will concentrate their minds,' transmitted Ilanna to Twiggy with a certain amount of glee.

'It certainly will, well jumped,' transmitted Twiggy back to Ilanna. Ilanna's ears which had been pinned back on her head were now pricked, and her tail which had been between her legs stood up proudly.

Quiviuk moved into the pack. Across the void Twiggy heard him asking the young and fit wolves to jump the gap, to show the others it could be done and to give them confidence.

Five big, young and fit looking wolves were jostling for position. The first one stood at the edge, he sniffed the air, he moved back into the pack and down into the tunnel, the others made a way for him.

He raced to the gap and leapt splendidly to the other side. He looked triumphantly at Ilanna, but she pretended not to notice his prowess.

The second jumped successfully over too. Pleased with themselves they stood on the other side, yapping and calling to the others.

As the third ran to make the jump, Twiggy felt Ilanna tense. 'He has not thrown his heart over,' she transmitted sadly.

Twiggy watched with horror as the wolf tried desperately to reach the other side. Its front claw scraped the rock face. But it was no good, the wolf disappeared into the void. It made no noise, immediately accepting its terrible fate. All the other wolves became silent. Only Twiggy and Jack cried out.

Now a fourth wolf lined up for a run up. He started bounding but at the last moment his courage failed and he tried to stop, but the rock was smooth and slippery. Part of him fell off the ledge, he scrambled frantically with his front legs. Quick as a flash Nick reached for the back of the wolf's neck, he heaved with all his might. The wolf made a last effort and both fell backwards onto the rock.

Jack looked at Nick incredulously. 'You just saved that wolf Nick,' he stated.

'I guess I did,' he said with a wan smile.

But now the last few wolves were anxious and afraid.

The she-wolves carrying Jack and Blue spoke up. They wanted to negotiate their freedom too. Quiviuk had no choice but to agree to their terms. He knew that he had to build the confidence of the other wolves again.

Twiggy held her breath watching her two friends Blue and Jack on their wolves trot back together to get a run up. They ran as a pair, leapt into the air and miraculously arrived on the other side. Blue and Jack looked shocked at what they had just experienced.

'Well done my sisters,' complimented Ilanna, 'But what about our mother?'

'She says she will go back to the other world, the man-cub is too heavy for her to carry across the gap,' replied the other she-wolves.
'Then she will die,' said Ilanna shortly.

'And the man-cub too,' agreed the smaller of the wolves.

Jack asked, 'What are they waiting for?'

'They're frightened and can't make the leap and oh Jack, if they go back they will die!' cried Twiggy desperately.

Jack suddenly had an idea. He exclaimed 'I know how to make the gap narrower, I've got to go back with my board.'

He called to Theta urgently to explain that he needed to return. Theta called to the wolf carrying him, but she had no intention of returning.

'How can you make it narrower?' asked Twiggy.

'I can use my board like a spring board, we can pin it down with a couple of boulders. It will work I know' said Jack excitedly. In her head Twiggy translated Jack's idea to Ilanna. Ilanna called the two she-wolves to her and softly transmitted what Twiggy had just said.

It was decided to take Jack back. Blue's wolf said that she would do it as she was the strongest. Jack and Blue swapped places. It was awful to see that Jack would have to do the dreadful leap again, and then a third time to come back, thought Twiggy to herself. But above all she admired the she-wolf who was to carry him.

'What's her name?' she transmitted to Ilanna.

'Ataaki,' silently replied Ilanna, 'She'll be safe: once she's decided that she is going to do something, she does not fail.' Even though she sounded confident, Twiggy could feel her tense as Ataaki ran in the opposite direction, leapt, and to everyone's relief landed with the Ravening wolves.

'So, young Jack,' said Theta 'What must we do?'

'If we put my board here,' said Jack putting the rounded tip on the edge of the ledge, 'then it sticks out into space and it'll be springy and give extra lift, we just have to wedge it firmly one end, with say a couple of big rocks on the corner…What?' He watched with amazement, as the board wiggled slightly in his hand and then the rounded corner settled into a perfectly shaped groove. 'Just as if it's made for it,' said Jack incredulously. 'There!' He gestured dramatically. 'You have a perfect spring board.'

The wolves and Theta looked at the board quivering slightly sticking straight out into space. They were not convinced. There was a pause then the mother wolf indicated to Nick that he was to climb on her back.

Nick hesitated.

'Nick this is no time to be a coward, everyone is watching, go for it!' commanded Jack.

Nick wanted to say, '*You* go for it,' but he could see that Jack's wolf was still trying to get her breath back.

They could all hear Nick muttering to himself, 'I'm really asleep. It's just a nightmare. I'll wake up, wake up, wake up…' as he climbed like a sleepwalker onto the mother wolf's back.

'Tell her to jump off the very end,' said Jack urgently to Theta. Theta translated his advice.

The mother wolf with Nick on her back went a little way into the tunnel to get a run up.

She came past more deliberately than the others, but her eyes were fixed on the snowboard. She ran onto it. Then there was horrible moment when the board dropped down with her weight and Nick's desperate cry could be heard above all the others. Then the board sprung up with a force that shot the mother wolf higher into space than all the others before her. She went so far that she landed beyond the ledge on the far side and disappeared a little way into the opposite tunnel. There was a 'Yikes!' from Nick as he tumbled off.

Now there was a scramble to test the springboard. Each wolf gave a delighted yelp as it was catapulted to the other side. Theta looked especially splendid with his greatcoat flying and his hairy limbs flailing the air.

At the end there were just two figures left.

'I can't leave my board, wolf,' said Jack willing the she-wolf to understand. To his great relief, it seemed she did understand. She watched Jack remove the helpful springboard without as much as a whine. The board came out of the groove easily. This really surprised Jack when he considered how, only moments before, it had supported the pack and Theta.

Ataaki went to make her run for the third time. Theta and Nick waiting at the point where they hoped Ataaki, with Jack on top, would land. Ready to give them help if they fell short.
There was stillness in the Ravening Pack, that contrasted with the mad dash and clatter of Ataaki's run to the edge, then they were both in the air and Ataaki was stretching for the other side. She landed hard on her chest and her breath was punched out of her. Jack would have fallen if it had not been for Theta's hand steadying him.

'Well done!' yelled Blue and Twiggy.

The Ravening Pack showed their admiration. Each wolf came up and made obeisance to Ataaki and many of them came and sidled past Jack too. Their ears were pinned back and their tails between their legs, indicating their subservience to Jack.

It was much later on that they came to the end of the tunnel and emerged high up and into a cold dawn. Theta commanded them to stop and rest. The pack dispersed into the wood close by and very soon they could be heard hunting. After a while Quiviuk returned with a haunch of bloody venison. Other wolves brought back fir cones and small branches at the command of Theta. They all had blood on their muzzles, where they had fed on a deer. Theta blew over the fir cones in his hands and muttered strange words. But the children were too tired to watch. Though they lifted their heads when they heard the sound of a fire crackling and the lovely smell of myrtle and juniper began to blow over the snow. He cut the venison into small steaks and offered the lightly seared meat to the children. It was delicious, fresh and juicy. They could feel the food giving them back their strength. Full of meat and absorbing the warmth from the fire they huddled around Theta and slept exhausted.

Chapter 11

Nick woke first. The midday sun was burning him. He sat up. He could clearly remember a terrible nightmare where he had clung onto the back of a wolf. He opened one eye warily, to his horror he could see that he was still experiencing his nightmare. It seemed he was still in the mountains and lying next to a fire. In the distance he could see three she-wolves, but that was all. He wondered where the others were.

Theta was huddled over the fire. On the fire was a small pot bubbling away cheerfully. Seeing Nick awake Theta tipped the pot and poured him a drink into a wooden mug. The drink was warming and enlivening. As each child woke the mug was refilled and passed around.

'Where did you find the pot and mug?' asked Twiggy.

'Where did you find the delicious soup?' asked Nick.

'From an old camp, the campers did not leave the place as they found it,' replied Theta his voice full of disapproval at the former owners.

 'Where are the rest of the wolves?' asked Blue.

'They have left us,' replied Theta shortly.

'Why?' asked Twiggy blowing on her mug to cool it down.

'They believe we are too slow and that they can find their way without us,' Theta shook his head sorrowfully. 'The Ravening Wolves are a proud and fierce race, but I do not believe that they will find the way through the Fault that will lead us to the far mountains of the Himalayas. Instead they will starve and be forced to hunt sheep, and then the men of this valley will hunt them and kill them.'

There was a small silence. Then Blue spoke up.

'Theta if you intend to go to the Himalayas,' she said speaking as politely as she could, 'we would rather you showed us the way to the men that you speak of. We are missing our parents and I'm sure that the people of this valley would be able to take us back to them. Our parents will be incredibly worried by now, you see.'

Theta looked at her without speaking for a long time. Perhaps he was trying to work out how the children would react when he gave them his answer, anyway he gave a deep sigh and said, 'There is no way out of this valley except the way we've come and I cannot return until I have regained my strength. I am getting weaker daily. The other way out is to commit ourselves to The Fault and it takes much courage to enter The Fault. No man in this valley has ever attempted it.'

Jack looked at Theta, was it his imagination or did Theta seem to be a bit smaller?

'Then how are we going to get back?' asked Twiggy in a small voice.

'I cannot foretell the future,' replied Theta in a kind voice. 'Whatever happens at the end, wherever that may be, I will strive to find a way to return you to your land. Now we need to move; the people here have a reputation of being fierce and unfriendly.'

'When you said the Himalayas, Theta,' started Nick, 'you must be wrong because the Himalayas are miles … more than miles...' he thought for a moment to think of a suitable word to impress Theta of the immense distance. 'They are whole continents away,' he pointed out.

'Not if you travel as I do,' answered Theta.

'Well,' said Nick 'I don't want to travel as you do. It's been awful so far. Blue is right we can't go on; we're certainly not coming to the Himalayas with you Theta. You must show us the way to a village, and we'll take our chances,' he said stubbornly. Nick looked at Blue and Twiggy, 'Won't we?'

Blue said doubtfully, 'There is no harm in having a look is there? What about you Jack?'

Jack did not answer, he had been lost in thought, but now he looked at Theta. 'Was it you I saw at the airport Theta?' he asked changing the subject. Theta nodded.

'How did you get here?' asked Twiggy surprised.

Jack gave a sudden start, 'Somehow you were in my backpack?'

'I am able to make myself very compact,' nodded Theta, 'but it takes a very great toll on my strength to keep changing size.'

There was a silence whilst Jack thought about how Theta had been with him all the time in his bag. It made him more determined to remain with Theta. But Blue persisted with her questioning,

'Perhaps while you have been away from this valley, the people have built a road out?' suggested Blue. 'I think you will find that since you have been in the attic, they will have become modern and have cars and internet.'

'I'm sure my dad will pay them,' interrupted Nick.

Blue continued, 'You don't have to come with us Theta; you can go on.'

'But I need Jack,' replied Theta. 'Only Jack has the power to ride his board Avalanche Rider. It is Jack and Avalanche Rider who are the key to sealing the ways that I have opened on my travels here. I must close the ways that have opened, otherwise the wrong men will follow us through and spoil our valleys.'

His voice quickened as he spoke, 'Blue my home valley is beautiful, but when I was a child I was bored with its beauty and decided to see other worlds. Then I travelled the mountains of your world. I was glad to see some of them. But many humans are greedy. They are unkind to the earth and make the air smell bad. There are many men who would use the natural resources in my land to fuel your cities. I *would* go alone but the power I had to close the hidden ways has all but gone.'

Blue looked at Jack and Theta with dismay, 'He's my little brother Theta, my mother and father would expect him to stay with me.'

'I'm going with Theta, Blue. Please come too,' said Jack simply.

'If you're both going, I'm coming too,' said Twiggy.

'Well I'm taking my chances with the people of this valley,' stated Nick firmly. 'I've had enough of this horrid nightmare and I'm going to get out of it somehow.'

Neither Nick nor Jack would change their mind. At last Blue suggested a compromise. They would all move stealthily to the edge of a village and keep out of sight. Then if Nick wanted to, he could continue into the village and see what it was like. At night, he could come back and tell the others whether he was staying, and if it was possible to get out of the valley. Theta did not contribute to the discussion. The she-wolves who had stayed with them left to hunt and came back with two mountain hares.

'I think I might have to go back to being a vegetarian,' said Blue faintly when she saw the beautiful creatures, their white pelts tinged with blood. She watched Theta efficiently skinning and cooking the hares.

'When we eat, we think with respect of the skill of the hunters and the goodness of the animals whose lives we have taken to save ours,' said Theta as he handed her a piece of rich meat, steaming in the cold mountain air. Blue chewed it with as much respect as she could muster.

As they moved into the afternoon and the sun started to go down, it quickly became chilly. Blue asked Theta to lead them to the closest village. Theta was doubtful about the wisdom of Nick going into the village, but agreed that there could be no harm in looking upon a village from a vantage point high up.

'Whatever we decide,' he pointed out, 'must happen quickly as I need to make a shelter for tonight. We go through The Fault at dawn tomorrow.'

Blue shivered when she heard these words. A cosy village sounded a much more attractive idea.

Theta went on, 'I cannot stay much longer in this valley. It is pulling at my powers and making me less strong.'

'What are the wolves going to do?' asked Twiggy.

'They will follow me as they want to enter The Fault. They know that it is only Jack and I who can show them the way,' replied Theta.

Surely we will be safe with Theta and the wolves, wished Twiggy to herself as they prepared to leave.

Blue, Nick and Twiggy put on their skiis and Nick his board. The snow was heavy and crusty, Jack skimmed over the top. Blue had to snow plough lightly without breaking the crust. *I wish I was on my board,* thought Twiggy. Nick was annoyed when he saw Jack leading and sped past him.

'This is a disaster waiting for a place to happen,' thought Blue to herself as she saw Nick taking on far too much speed. Not a moment later there was a cry and Nick plunged hard into the ground and then slipped on down the slope, making a great deal of noise.

They all grouped round the fallen figure. Only the she-wolves keeping their distance. Nick was hunched over clutching his arm.

'I've broken my wrist' he gulped. Theta moved to his side and went to touch his wrist, his huge hairy hand reaching out to Nick.

'What do you think you're doing? Don't touch me!' he yelled at Theta.

Theta paused, he held out his hand, his palm towards Nick's wrist, and kept it there for a moment. 'Your wrist is not broken; it is lightly strained. There is some heat. In a moment even that will be gone,' he pronounced.

'You're not a doctor,' Nick grumbled. 'Anyway, my hands are freezing, these gloves are no good, I lost my best ones,' he added mournfully.

'Put your hands out in front of me and I can give you warmth for a short while,' said Theta patiently.

'Do as he says, and don't be so rude,' demanded Twiggy.

Nick must have been at the end of his tether, for he meekly put out his hands. Theta put his palms above Nick's. Nick winced slightly then looked astonished when a delicious warmth flooded not only through his hands, but into the very core of his body.

'That's better,' he said and then ashamedly he stammered, 'thank you.'

He got up. 'I'm going to have to walk to the village,' he told them, 'I can't ski this stuff; it's too difficult.'

'Don't be silly Nick,' answered Blue. 'The snow's too deep to walk. Anyway you fell because you were going too fast.'

'Nick you will ski beside me and I will give you balance. Come we must keep going; it will be dark soon,' said Theta. Nick did as he was told and while he kept close to Theta he felt as though he had perfect balance. Theta loped over the snow easily with one arm pointing at Nick.

It's as if he has Nick on a lead thought Blue fascinated. Sometimes Theta would wave an arm over all of them and as long as they stayed close to him, they all felt much more confident. As the sun dropped the temperature did too. A wan moon lit the frozen fields as they slipped over the snowy crust, dropping towards lights they could see twinkling below.

'I've never skied so fast or so well!' gasped Blue to herself delightedly. She glanced across at Jack as he boarded by her. They grinned maniacally at each other.

Meanwhile Twiggy found Ataaki running beside her. 'This is wonderful!' she transmitted to Ataaki.

'Running with the pack is always exhilarating,' agreed Ataaki silently to her. Twiggy felt that she never wanted the moment to end. She wanted to ski with wolves for ever.

Chapter 12

Theta held up his hand and they all came to a sudden stop. There was a ledge in front of them and below it, they could see a clear track. They could smell wood smoke. Theta crept stealthily to the ledge and motioned for Blue to join him. Twiggy noticed that the wolves had disappeared into the woods.

The village was small, but towards its centre they could hear cries and see the glow of a great bonfire. Occasionally sparks spat into the night sky. Close by they could see that the houses were mostly made of wood with some stone, like the ones in their skiing village. Logs were neatly piled up under windows. On the ground floor of one house there was a stable. An old horse poked his head over the top of the door and blew hard through his nostrils.

'Perhaps he scented the wolves,' said Theta quietly. 'We stop here.'

'I wish I wasn't going by myself,' Nick said miserably looking at the dark houses. 'I don't speak French!'

Blue felt uncomfortable. To her it did seem wrong that just one of them was going to suddenly appear in the village.

'Perhaps I'd better come too; there's bound to be some English tourists there.' She looked at Theta for his reaction.

'I think you should follow at a distance and try and assess the villagers' mood,' he warned.

'What happens if they're unfriendly?' asked Blue.

'Are there more villages?' asked Nick 'Is this the best one?'

'I have only travelled through here once but I have listened to what I have been told by the wolves, owls and eagles and by other Mountain People. They do talk about more than one village, but the other would be further down the valley, this is the highest.' He went on. 'I don't believe they would harm one of their own; I only fear that once you are with them you can never leave.'

'I'll come just a little bit further with you,' said Blue to Nick.

Blue waved Nick forward, 'What do you think?' she asked.

Nick could hear the big bonfire and voices. He thought of a comfortable bed, internet and television. How would wolves, owls and eagles know anything about technology, he scoffed to himself. To him Theta seemed hopelessly primitive.

He said determinedly, 'I still want to try. I don't know how people can exist if there is no contact with the outside world, I just can't believe it.' He shivered, 'I've had enough of this adventure *anything* would be better than what we've just been through.'

He put his skiis against a rock. 'Goodbye you lot,' he said, 'I think you're mad not to come with me. What messages will I give your parents?' he asked.

It was that last sentence that persuaded Blue to go too, she could not bear to think that the village below them might have someone who could lead them back to Méribel. She could not bear to think how anxious her mother would be if, and when, Nick told her that she had gone through a 'Fault' with Theta.

'I'll come just a little bit further with you,' repeated Blue to Nick.

'Jack?' asked Blue.

Jack shook his head, 'I believe Theta, Blue, but I'm going to wait here so that you can come back and tell me that you're safe. If you don't come back, I'll come and get you.'

'How will I find you? You can't stay here all night or you'll freeze,' worried Blue.

'I can make a small cave in the woods,' said Theta. 'Be assured Blue, we leave at dawn.'

'Oh dear, I just don't know what to do,' said Blue in a small voice.

'Make a noise like an owl when you come back,' said Jack, 'but if there is danger cough, OK?'

On cue in the woods an owl cried making everyone start. They laughed nervously.
'Like that Blue, OK?' said Jack. Blue nodded, but now it was nearly dark and all he could see was her wool hat going backwards and forwards.

'Dad'll kill me if I turn up without you,' said Blue.

'If you find we can get out of this valley then I'll come too,' agreed Jack and Twiggy nodded. Hearing this Theta turned away, they could feel his disappointment, making Jack feel very torn.

Nick started to climb down the bank. He was anxious to get back to civilisation. Blue followed, leaving her skis and poles neatly on the ledge. They trudged along the track which zigzagged its way down below Theta, Jack and Twiggy. They arrived at the edge of the village where, after a whispered consultation, Nick moved ahead of Blue and started to walk up the street. Blue followed stealthily, darting from doorway to doorway until they went out of sight of the watchers. The village looked charming, there were no street lights, just light from the big moon, and flickering yellow light from the bonfire ahead. What was odd was there were no cars.

Out of sight Theta, Jack and Twiggy peered into the gloom. They knew when Nick arrived in the middle of the village for there was a sudden hush followed by a terrific clamour of voices and shouting. It was difficult to tell whether they could hear anger, surprise or excitement.

'Has he done the right thing?' asked Twiggy nervously.

'He never does the right thing,' replied Jack shortly. But now *he* was very worried that *he* had not done the right thing by Blue. After all he was her brother, he should have gone with her. He looked around to see what Theta was thinking, but Theta had moved back into the trees and was looking for shelter. They could see his shape moving back and forth. When he stopped moving he looked exactly like a rock, and then Jack and Twiggy strained to see him, and worried that they had been abandoned.

After ten cold minutes he came out of the wood and led them to the shelter he had made, it was a snow hole and when they had crawled into it, Theta gave them each a stone to hold onto. The stone radiated heat right into their hearts. It warmed their bodies and made them feel re-energised.

'How did you do that Theta?' asked Twiggy admiringly. 'This is lovely,' she said hugging her stone. Then Ataaki crept into the snow hole and sat by Twiggy. 'How wonderful I've got double central heating now!'

In the village Nick's spirits started to rise as he got nearer to the noise of people enjoying themselves. He marched down the street with excited anticipation, he knew Blue was following behind trying to keep out of sight and this gave him added confidence.

Blue however, was not enjoying her journey. Every time she stopped in the low cramped doorways a rat would scamper from under her feet, or a baleful cat sitting on a window sill would hiss angrily at her. When the first rat jumped up from her foot, she had been unable to stop herself from giving a little shriek.
'Why aren't the cats catching the rats?' she thought to herself.

'What's the matter,' shushed Nick turning.

'There are rats everywhere,' she whispered.

'Don't be pathetic,' replied Nick.

Not only was there a rat in every doorway, but there was a bad smell of dead animal. Halfway up the street, she intuitively felt that there was something dreadfully wrong about the village.

'Nick,' she hissed, 'Nick come back.' But it was too late: at that moment Nick stepped into the village square.

Chapter 13

Nick stepped into the bonfire's light. He could see the silhouetted shapes of many children standing round the bonfire. The bonfire was built round a burning figure.

'Guy Fawkes night,' thought Nick delightedly. But at that moment he realised that the figure was not a straw stuffed scarecrow, but an animal. To his horror Nick recognised Quiviuk the leader of the Ravening Pack. Instinctively he looked round to shield Blue from the terrible sight. Too late he could see her pale face caught by the light of the bonfire. She had forgotten to hide as she stood, eyes huge with outrage, staring at the dead wolf. Then suddenly she started and dived again into the shadows.

Someone had noticed Nick and with shouts of frenzied excitement all the children turned. Nick saw however, that they were not children but small humans of middle age or older, and they quickly surrounded him.

'Ahem hello, good evening, good evening,' stuttered Nick instinctively holding up his hands as if someone was pointing a gun at him. 'Does anyone speak English, speek Eenglish?' he asked plaintively. He could not get the picture of Quiviuk out of his mind. As he spoke there was a sudden shushing and part of the crowd made way for a woman to come forward. She looked Nick up and down. There was a silence from everybody else.

'Is the war finished?' she asked. She had to repeat this question twice before Nick could understand it.

Nick wished that he read the newspapers more often. He had absolutely no idea what she was talking about.

'There are no wars around here as far as I know and there haven't been for a very long time,' he replied.

She looked at him balefully, as she translated back to those who could not understand.

'How did you get here?' asked another old woman with the same guttural accent.

'Through a tunnel,' answered Nick.

'How did you get across the abyss?' asked another. Here Nick could not answer. He could not say that he jumped it on the back of a wolf, when his nostrils were full of the foul smell of the death of Quiviuk. They saw his hesitation. Several more yelled questions.

'How did you find your way through the labyrinth?'

'You must tell us now,' demanded the first crone.

'I-, I jumped,' said Nick.

'You are a liar,' spat the crone. 'Now!' she cried, and in seconds ropes were thrown round Nick, which circled round his legs. The men and women who had thrown them pulled sharply on the lassoos and Nick's legs were pulled from underneath him. Down he went.

In the shadows Blue watched the proceedings with horror. She pressed her back against the log wall between the door and the window and tried to make herself very small.

As she stood there trembling, to her shock, right next to her face the window moved outwards. Mesmerised with fear Blue could not move and she watched helplessly as a face looked into hers ... eyeball to eyeball.

'Please don't hurt me,' she begged and she was aware that tears were slipping down her cheeks.

'I won't, but there's plenty that will,' purred a voice in her head. 'Move slowly to the door and I'll let you in.' After a desperate glance at the crowd milling round the yelling Nick, Blue edged under the porch and put her back to the door, which opened suddenly, and she crept inside.

The main light came from outside. A yellow light sent by the flames from the bonfire flickered, sometimes weakly and sometimes more brightly through the windows, giving Blue occasional glimpses of the room that she had stepped into. The room had a low ceiling with many blackened beams separated by tiles running parallel across its entirety. In one part were a table and chairs and in the other a chair in front of a range. The range had a little window in its door and through the panes, one of which was broken, Blue could see the dying embers of a fire. It was this that made the room warm.

In the poor light Blue could just make out the pale shape of the creature that had let her in, it seemed to be a huge cat which came up to Blue's waist. She stood still trying to stop her teeth chattering whilst the creature sniffed her. Its whiskers tickled her hands and she felt strangely reassured and began to relax a little.

'You are a female like I am.' It transmitted silently to her. 'I have never come across one so young, I think you are the same age as I.'

Blue froze when she heard the voice in her head. So, this is what Twiggy was experiencing when she spoke with the wolves.

'Can you really understand me?' she worried to herself, 'What's going to happen to me?'

'I'm afraid they will come for you,' replied the big cat answering both questions.

'But no one saw me,' replied Blue, speaking in her head.

'One of the cats or rats will tell someone - they cannot all be trusted,' the big cat told her. 'How did you get here?' Blue could hear a desperate longing in her voice.

'I came through a tunnel,' she replied. She remembered the language of the villagers when they questioned Nick. She explained, 'What you call the labyrinth and then over the abyss.' 'Oh!' exclaimed the big cat disappointedly, 'then you will not escape, there is no way out of here.'

'But there is,' said Blue suddenly putting all her trust into the big cat. 'We are with Theta, who is going to lead us into something called The Fault and that will take us to another world.'

'Theta?' breathed the cat, 'Who is Theta?'

'Theta is a mountain man. I think he is like a yeti, but I've never met a yeti, so I don't know exactly. He has special powers, he can talk to the wolves and he can make light,' explained Blue in a rush.

'I believe this is a man of my valley, the Valley of Songinvelo,' purred the big cat. 'What is your name?' it asked.

'Blue,' she answered. 'And yours?'

But now the cat stopped purring and said, 'I have forgotten my real name. I don't know how my mother and I came into this valley - perhaps through The Fault. I remember powerful arrows falling around us. I got separated from my mother and was captured. I believe she was shot. I never saw her again.'

Blue could see the big cat's eyelids close for a moment. The cat continued, 'My mother called me 'kitten' and 'little piece of the moon', but I have grown away from the names of childhood.'

'Do you live here alone?' asked Blue. The big cat shook its head and told her that she lived with a kindly old lady who had taken pity on the spitting kitten that the men had brought back from their hunt.

'She is different from the others, she doesn't encourage the rats, in fact quite the reverse, I control them for her,' said the cat, and Blue could hear the cat's tongue lick its lips. 'I call her Aunt May' and the big cat stretched and continued, 'She protects the birds' eggs from the rest of the villagers, otherwise we would have no more swallows or swifts. They have killed all the local birds; they eat everything they can find.'

'Will they eat the wolf and …Nick?' asked Blue horrified.

'They will eat the wolf tonight yes, as for Nick, if you mean the man cub, they will eat him when they can find no more use for him. First he will have to do the jobs they can no longer do.'

'Like what?' asked Blue.

'When I saw him pass by I thought he looked strong and young, so he can mend the roofs and bring in the wood; their strength is failing, but not their cunning,' answered the big cat.

Blue wondered how helpful Nick would be. She had her doubts.

'I don't think it will be very long before Nick is eaten. I must save him somehow and get him back to Theta,' she looked at the big cat, who looked away. 'Can you help me?' she begged.

'I will try but I do not know how. If I succeed, will you take me to Theta and The Fault?' agreed the cat.

'Yes I will but oh, they leave for The Fault at dawn, and worse if I don't go back, my little brother Jack will come and look for me; then he'll get captured!'
'Dawn?' exclaimed the cat, 'but that is in only a few hours. I must find out what has happened to your Nick. You must hide. Some of the villagers speak rat. I don't think it will be long before they come looking for you.' The cat looked around and then told Blue to hide on a wide shelf.

'Get under the skins, this is where I usually lie. Do not move. I will be back.'

The cat opened the door and slipped out noiselessly. Peeping between the skins Blue watched its great shape. There was a moment when the light outside illuminated the cat.

'But that's not a cat at all!' she gasped to herself 'How wonderful, it's a snow leopard!' The leopard gave her the briefest of glances and then shut the door.

It was not difficult to find Nick, he was being force fed gruel. It was a thin soup that the villagers relied on in the winter. The vegetable stock was never served to the last drop, it was constantly added to. Every home made their special brew. In autumn the soup might consist of mushrooms and herbs and could be delicious, but in winter when it was difficult to find anything to put in it, the soup was thickened with bark and lichen. Nick was not enjoying it.

'Stop giving it to me,' he spluttered. 'It's disgusting.'

'What an unpleasant, fussy and rude boy!' scolded the Dame who as the leading matriarch of the village had taken it upon herself to house Nick. She was already regretting her decision.

'Untie me now or my father will sue you.' Nick had practised this remark many times. Here it was an idle threat. The Dame merely slapped Nick hard in the face and told him to be quiet or something worse would happen.

As Nick was still tied up there was little he could do. One of his eyes watered on the side of the slap, which had left a red weal. He blinked the tears away and said to the Dame, 'You cannot imagine how much trouble you're in.' As he was speaking the Dame picked up a length of material and twisted it. Nick did not notice and carried on, 'I've got friends in high places not to mention Thet. . .' but in the middle of his sentence the Dame gagged Nick there and then, which was lucky as otherwise he would have told her all about Theta and the wolves. His eyes bulged and he tried to kick the Dame. For the Dame this was the last straw. She snatched up her walking stick from behind the door and hit Nick about the shoulders and legs and once on the head for good measure.

The snow leopard was watching through the window and she winced as she saw the blows fall upon Nick. She trotted back through the dark. Suddenly a group of villagers hobbled up the street. They ignored the leopard as they saw her daily. They made their way as fast as they could to the Dame's house. With her heart sinking, the leopard turned around and trotted back after them.

The little group barged their way through the Dame's door. Each one intent on being the first to give her the news.

'There's another one in the village!' they exclaimed.

'A girl!' informed one.

'Attractive, not like this one,' pointed out another.

'Where?' demanded the Dame.

'We don't know; she's disappeared,' they replied.

'Well find her!' shrieked the Dame. 'Wake the village, bribe the rats, do what you must, but find the girl.'

The group made small bobs and curtseys. 'Yes Dame Malintention, right away Dame Malintention,' they cried and rushed out again.

Nick in the depths of his misery did not understand the language they had spoken. But their gesticulations and the Dame's furious response had spoken volumes. Someone had obviously seen Blue and now they were off to find her, and if they found her, then he and she were sunk. Theta, Jack, Twiggy and the wolves would disappear into The Fault and he and Blue would have to live in this drear and unkind village for the rest of their days.

The snow leopard made her way back to Aunt May's house where she lived. Aunt May was already back and she had put the kettle on and her own gruel concoction (much nicer than Dame Malintention's) was simmering next to the kettle. There was no sign of Blue. Aunt May looked round as the leopard padded in. 'Hello lovely puss, been hunting have you?'

The leopard put her head gently on Aunt May's shoulder for a moment. 'Well, that's a lovely thing. You've never done that before; what's got into you puss, eh?' said Aunt May touched, she scratched the leopard behind its ears. 'That's right you lie down' she said to the leopard as she leapt onto the ledge and settled carefully round the hidden Blue.

'Do not speak aloud Blue,' warned the leopard.

'Did you find Nick?' transmitted Blue breathlessly for she was somewhat squashed by the leopard's paw.

'I did. He is tied up and I cannot untie the knots. Somehow I have to get you to him but everyone is looking for you.'

'What if they find me?' asked Blue. 'Perhaps it would be better to get help. I could leave the village and find Theta.'

'It's further out of the village than it is to where Nick is tied up,' said the leopard. 'We need to see what happens and then I will make a plan.'

Already the village which was just settling down after the excitement of the bonfire was reawakening to search for a girl. Occasionally there would be a high-pitched shrieking, and a rat would run past the window, its nose twitching as it followed Blue's scent.

'Now what?' muttered Aunt May as a terribly loud knocking battered at her door. 'What do you want?' she cried.

She did not like her routine altered and as far as she was concerned, she had had enough excitement already, what with that miserable bonfire and the tragic wolf, and then a boy arriving in the middle of the 'festivities'.

Three men piled into the room. 'The rats have followed the scent of a girl as far as your house Aunt May,' they informed her. 'We believe she might be hiding in here,' they added.

'In here?' retorted Aunt May. 'Don't be ridiculous young Crabby, I would have seen a girl if she was in here,' she scoffed.

'Beggin' your pardon Aunt May, but we have orders to search every house, and especially yours.'

The Dame suddenly made an entrance. 'What's the problem?' she demanded imperiously. 'Search the house and be quick about it. Leave no stone unturned.' She looked defiantly at Aunt May, there was no love lost between the two old women. The men clumped up the stairs.

'The disrespect of them going through my things! Just you wait you boys,' called Aunt May after the men who were sixty if they were a day. She trotted nimbly after them, belying her eighty-five years of age.

The Dame remained downstairs and listened to the men searching Aunt May's bedroom. Her eyes wandered round the room and lit on the leopard. The leopard and the Dame stared at each other for a moment and then the leopard started disinterestedly washing its foot.

'How she can live with that great fur ball, I just don't know,' muttered the Dame with distaste. She bent down to look under the table.

The men clumped back downstairs again. They looked red-faced and embarrassed. They shook their heads at the Dame. One of them said defensively to Aunt May, 'It was the rats what led us here.'

'The rats!' exclaimed Aunt May. 'As if you can trust a rat, especially as the rats hate my big cat. I bet they enjoyed trying to put the blame on this house. What an utter waste of time! I don't believe there even is a girl if you got your information from rats. Why don't you ask the boy if there is one?'

Blue tensed when she heard Aunt May say this. What would Nick's answer be? Would he tell the Dame the whereabouts of the others?

As the men and the Dame left, another yell started in the village.

'We've seen more wolves! We're going to track them down,' called three women to the Dame.

'Which direction?' she asked excitedly.

'North,' they replied.

'Wait whilst I get my poisoned arrows,' screeched the Dame 'Have you let the other villages know?' she asked. But she needed no answer, for in the distance they could hear a horn calling the other villages. Then a tune was played on the horn to indicate which direction the other villagers should take, so that they could encircle the wolves.

Reindeer were being pulled from stables and harnessed to sledges. Men and women appeared carrying an assortment of spears, bows and arrows, and ancient guns.

'I'm coming, don't start without me,' ordered the Dame as she returned quickly to her house to fetch her bow and poison-tipped arrows.

As they heard the swish of sledges through the slush, the leopard leapt lightly to the floor. Aunt May had gone upstairs.

'This is our chance to get your friend,' she purred. Blue followed quickly and the two crept to the door.

'Keep to one side of me, and if anyone passes hide by my shoulder,' the leopard commanded.

Stooping low, Blue ran beside the trotting leopard.

'I see you, I see you, and I'm going to tell!' she heard a small excited voice screech. A rat darted in front of them.

'Oh no you're not!' exclaimed the leopard, and she pounced on the rat and bit it once, then discarded the body.

'Oh dear!' said Blue faintly as she stepped over the spots of blood on the snow.

The snow leopard led her to the Dame's house and in they went.

'I can't see anything,' whispered Blue to the leopard. Then she heard muffled cries coming from the gagged Nick. Blue groped her way to the voice. She patted down Nick until she found the knots and being rather efficient at that sort of thing, she quickly undid all of them, bar one.

'This one is so tight; could you bite it off?' she transmitted to the leopard.

To Nick she said, 'Don't be afraid Nick. I've got a leopard to help me and she's going to bite the knot off.'

'I don't care what's helping you, just get me out of here, I think they're going to kill me,' he moaned. The leopard neatly bit the knot and the rope fell off Nick. He moved stiffly into a standing position.

'That horrible woman beat me with a stick,' he told Blue. 'I can't see out of one eye and my nose is agony.'

'Poor you,' said Blue 'Hold my hand and I'll lead you out, then we must run beside the leopard and duck down if anyone comes.'

'Oh hell,' said Nick when they were outside and the light was better. 'You really *do* mean a leopard.' He thought for a moment and then asked wearily to no one in particular, 'Why am I surprised?'

The main street was empty once more and they were able to run straight down it. In the distance high on the mountain, they could see lights and hear a horn blown urgently.

'What do you think they are hunting?' Blue asked. The leopard listened to the sound of the baying hounds. 'Not wolves, their notes sound uncertain. I'm afraid they may be hunting your Mountain Man.'

'Not Theta, oh no,' cried Blue.

They emerged from the village and Blue was suddenly confused and unsure of which track they had come from, but luckily Nick recognised a tree and a rock which was an odd shape. As they trudged up the path Blue remembered to hoot like an owl. To their enormous relief there were lots of hoots back and Twiggy and Jack emerged from the black, flinging themselves on Blue.

Twiggy suddenly noticed the leopard behind Nick. Lit by the moon she looked majestic.

'She's a friend,' explained Blue and went on hurriedly, 'Where's Theta?'

'He's creating a diversion. He sent Ataaki to go and look for you, but someone saw her and set the hounds on her and so Theta is trying to save her. He says we must follow the other wolves; he's told them where to go, we've got to leave now,' said Jack urgently.

Blue transmitted all this to the leopard. The leopard spoke in a different language to the she-wolves. She could not understand their answer. The leopard told Blue that a leopard and wolves would not usually travel together, but these were strange circumstances, and they had agreed to settle their traditional dislike of each other whilst there was so much danger.

It was an odd little group that stumbled off in the darkness to climb the mountain. They climbed through the trees where the snow was not so deep and they could pull themselves up by grabbing branches - but the going was pitifully slow.

Eventually Ilanna came back to Twiggy and offered to carry Nick. 'Why Nick, Ilanna? He should be the strongest. Is he just making his usual fuss?' she transmitted.

'No, this boy is suffering; he has many bruises and a broken bone in his face,' said Ilanna who could tell all this by sniffing the air.

Then Twiggy felt very ashamed. She called softly to Nick and told him that Ilanna would carry him. 'Thank you, thank you very much Ilanna,' said Nick gratefully to the wolf.

The snow leopard watched gravely as she saw Ilanna sag under his weight. Then the leopard, calling to Illanna in their special language, said that she could do the job more easily. She had to use very diplomatic language because the wolves were proud.

But Ilanna agreed immediately and arranged to carry Twiggy who was the smallest.

Nick got off Ilanna and climbed onto the snow leopard's magnificent back. Blue got behind him and Jack behind her. A she-wolf led the group and another brought up the rear. Now they could move much faster. Jack had his board, but they agreed to leave the others' skis and boards behind.

Under the beautiful leopard pelt, they could feel her muscles straining to carry them up the steep mountain side. It was nearly an hour later when they reached the place where Theta had told the she-wolves to go. They climbed off the leopard's back. The leopard immediately flopped to the ground panting hard.

The place where they had stopped was out of the wind. There was a flat area around which there were rock steps running up in a semi-circle. It looked like a Roman amphitheatre. Oddly there was no snow and they could hear a low moan from the ground. In the middle of the flat area there was a huge hole and warm air, which had melted all the snow, flowed out of it.

Jack picked his way carefully to the edge of the hole. His board thrummed in his hand. He clutched it tight.

'Is this The Fault?' he wondered as he stared down in to the dark.

'Be careful Jack,' warned Blue as she watched Jack looking into the void. Jack walked back to her. They looked at each other wearily, too tired to speak more.

Twiggy persuaded Nick to come a little closer to the warm air. She was being very solicitous. Nick was answering politely, but it was clear that he was exhausted and ached all over. The she-wolves circled the hole warily. The leopard stood by Blue sniffing and listening to the sounds on the night air. Blue thought she looked so beautiful with the moonlight falling upon her.

In the distance they could still hear the hunt, but now it was coming closer. The wolves growled with their ears pointed towards the sound. They spoke to each other, transmitting their thoughts so that no one could understand them except for Twiggy and the leopard.

Twiggy translated to Blue, Jack and Nick, 'They say that the hounds are hunting two creatures, which is confusing them. They believe that one is Theta and the other Ataaki. Ataaki and Theta keep running over each other's tracks and the hounds run into each other.'

The noise of the crying hounds came closer as did the sounds of the horns. Now even the children could hear the noise of people shouting and, every so often, a whip cracking.

Suddenly Ataaki appeared high up on the top-most step; her silhouette clear against the midnight blue of the horizon. She paused for a moment, her head low. Even as a silhouette it was possible to see her flanks heaving. Seeing her sisters she leapt from step to step to the stage below to join them. They came forward to greet her, followed by Twiggy who was aghast to see her friend so utterly exhausted. Immediately behind her came

Theta but he was much smaller, and instead of looking strong he looked very vulnerable.

'Jack, Jack hold Avalanche Rider above The Fault!' he called urgently as he ran.

'It's too dangerous!' cried out Blue. 'Can't you do it for him Theta?' she wailed.

Theta shook his head panting. He took Blue's hand, 'Little lady, I would if I could, but only Jack can wield Avalanche Rider.'

'What am I looking for?' called Jack back to Theta. The moment he had heard Theta's command he had rushed to The Fault and was already holding the board over the void.

'You will see the signs truly lit!' exclaimed Theta, 'When Jack gives the command - and not before - we must jump into The Fault, but whatever you do,' he shouted at everybody above the terrible noise of the hounds and the cries of the hunters who were nearly upon them, 'you must be touching Jack, or you must be touching somebody who is touching Jack.' And he turned towards the first hound which was right now leaping over the back of the amphitheatre. He called over his shoulder, 'Tell the wolves Twiggy!'

Twiggy translated all he had said to Ataaki in a garbled message. She was transfixed by the ghastly sight of the approaching hound. This was not like any hound that she had ever seen. At home she had patted a hound on the head and it had put two paws on her shoulders and given her a slobbery lick. This was something quite different. For a start it was twice the size, probably reaching to Twiggy's shoulder, and it looked mad with blood lust.

Despite its vicious mien, as one, the she-wolves banded together to face the lead hound. It stopped and howled back to the rest of the pack to let them know that it had found its quarry.

'What a coward you are, waiting for your friends. Afraid to attack?' snarled Ilanna.

As the wolf taunt rang out, Twiggy quailed, terrified that the hound would be pushed to attack the brave, but apparently foolhardy, she-wolves.

Ataaki, still panting hard beside Twiggy transmitted, 'Our only hope is to fight them one by one.'.

Ilanna's taunt worked; the hound leapt upon the she-wolf. As one, her mother and sisters rushed to her defence. The others watched in horror as terrible snarls and yelps pierced the night air. In the distance, it was possible to hear the oncoming baying of the rest of the pack drawing ever nearer.

Behind the melee, Jack was having an extraordinary experience with his board Avalanche Rider. Sometimes the patterns would shine purple and his board would push him back from the hole with apparent horror, and sometimes they would be partly green and the board would bring him back teetering on the edge. Once the patterns had flashed crimson and the board had thrummed in his hands angrily. Jack used all his concentration to watch the patterns and try to understand what he was to do. His wrists ached from the strain of holding on to his excited board. He was aware that Blue was holding on to the end of his jacket and this reassured him a little, until she cried, 'They're getting closer! Do something Jack!'

I'm trying, he thought desperately to himself, but he could not imagine what it *was* exactly … that he was meant to be doing.

Meanwhile things were going badly for the she-wolves, Blue screamed as she saw that the hound was going to tear the throat out of Ilanna. Her scream galvanised the snow leopard. She sprung from Blue's side straight onto the back of the vicious hound. Her top lip turned back revealing a set of immaculate weapons. She plunged two deadly pointed canines into the neck of the hound, killing it instantly.

There was no time to exult. On the topmost steps the rest of the hound pack arrived. They paused, as they had witnessed the leopard killing their biggest hound, and now waited for the reindeer and the sleighs with the hunters aboard to catch up and give them instructions. They did not have long to wait.

A sleigh arrived pulled by reindeer. These docile creatures were a sorry sight. Their flanks were heaving and there were weals on their backs where they had been whipped by Dame Malintention. The leather braces that tied them to the sleigh were frayed thin by being rubbed on the rocks as they hunted through the crags and corries of the mountains. Theta and Ataaki had certainly led them on a wild dance.

But Dame Malintention was buoyed by adrenalin. She screamed, 'Kill them!'

No sooner had her words ended on a high shriek, than the hounds and she acted. She lifted her whip and the sure-footed reindeer began to pick their way down the maze of square hewn stones. The hounds were far quicker; they slithered down the amphitheatre making light work of the unevenness, now much braver because their mistress was with them.

As they poured into the amphitheatre, several things happened at once. One of the lines of Dame Malintention's sleigh broke, skewing her sleigh at an angle and throwing her unceremoniously into the maze of stones. The reindeer kept on coming, frightened by the unbalanced jolting sleigh behind them, and they skidded to a halt, teetering on the precipice of The Fault. Dame Malintention struggled to her feet; she still had her bow in her hand and with her other she reached for a poisoned arrow. She stood tall and took aim at Theta.

Theta called out in desperation to Jack, 'Wield Avalanche Rider.'

Jack screwed his eyes up tight and willed Avalanche Rider to find the right place. But while he was concentrating he heard a horrible 'thump' and a cry - Theta had been hit by the poisoned arrow. Jack had little time to react, his board started tugging at him. The abyss was lit up with a golden light with glints of green. It looked beautiful. Jack understood that this was the moment.

He yelled, 'Now!' and his board began to teeter on the edge of the void.

The reindeer trotted right up to Blue who grabbed a rein. 'Pull Theta into the sleigh now' she commanded Nick. For the first time in his life Nick obeyed an order immediately. But it was not difficult to pull Theta into the sleigh because he was diminishing in size, as the poison coursed through his veins and he was in danger of disappearing completely.

'Get in!' Blue yelled to Twiggy and Nick. 'Snow leopard come to me now,' she transmitted as strongly as she could. 'Bring the she-wolves.'

Nick was already in the sleigh, but Twiggy could not leave Ataaki and all of the she-wolves were still desperately fighting. Just as she knew she would have to stay behind and fight, a tremendous howl came from behind her and the hounds glanced up.

'Its Quiviuk's pack!' screamed Twiggy with elation. The male wolves arrived determined to avenge Quiviuk. Thrusting the brave but exhausted she-wolves aside, they leapt into battle.

'Hurry!' yelled Jack 'I can't hold on much longer.'

The Snow leopard bounded to Blue's side.

'Hold me,' said Blue through her mind. As she felt the snow leopard gently put her jaws round her arm, Blue tightened her hold on Jack. Her other hand held the reins, she saw that Nick was helping a wounded she-wolf into the sleigh. Twiggy and the other wolves were scrambling over its side, as the sleigh started to tip, wolves that were not in the sleigh grabbed the tails of the ones who were.

Blue had hardly got the word 'Go!' out of her mouth, when she was jerked backwards off her feet and felt herself falling into warm air.

'Is Theta all right?' called Jack, but if there was an answer, he could not hear it, so great was the rushing wind past his ears. Eventually he lost all sensation other than his wrists locked round the edge of his board which thrummed and hummed delightedly, as it rode the wild currents of The Fault.

Chapter 14

Sometime later Jack was aware that they had stopped travelling. It was dark but he felt ground beneath him. He sighed with relief and fell into a deep sleep.

When Jack woke the sun was on his cheek. He felt entirely rested. It was not until he moved slightly that he realised that his wrists ached. And as he tried to stretch, he noticed that it was not only his wrists that ached, but his back, arms and legs.

He opened his eyes slowly. He seemed to be in a little cave. He could see out of the entrance, and in front and below him was a waterfall. He raised himself onto his elbow and was delighted to see Twiggy in the stream. She was playing in the water wearing only her vest and pants as a makeshift swimming costume and the she-wolves were gambolling and paddling beside her.

'Twiggy?' he called weakly. But it was Blue who answered, popping her head round the entrance.

'I thought you would never wake up! How are your arms?' she asked. At that Jack stretched his arms in front of him. He saw that they had been carefully bandaged. He could see herbs sticking out underneath the ends of the bandages.

'What happened?' he asked.

'Your wrists were terribly bruised. You were so brave to keep holding onto Avalanche Rider, Jack. You saved us all. One of the women here has put something healing on your wrists and I can see that the swelling has already gone.'

Jack flexed his fingers gingerly. 'They do ache a bit, but they don't feel seriously painful. What do you mean one of the women?'

He looked up as a woman walked in. She was dressed in a costume that reminded him of a picture in his geography book. He struggled to remember where in the world the woman in the picture lived. She patted Jack on the back and handed him a hot drink. Just sniffing the delicious concoction made his blood feel stronger. He moved into a sitting position.

'How long have we been here?' he asked.

'Some days, I think. We landed beside this village and the people seem really kind. They have been looking after us, but Jack I'm finding it impossible to keep track of time. It seemed like we were in The Fault for all of our lifetime, but that we have been here for only minutes. It's totally confusing, and though its lovely here, I really want to go home,' she finished forlornly and she buried her head into a large animal that had materialised beside her.

'Gosh, is that a snow leopard?' asked Jack in amazement and then he shook his head, 'Now I remember the escape from the village and you turning up with this leopard and Nick. Where is Nick?' he asked excitedly as all the memories of their adventures came rushing back to him.

'Nick has been plaguing the villagers with questions about how we get out of this *nightmare*, as he keeps describing it. But they have been so kind and gentle, that he just sounds ungrateful.'

'Theta! What happened to Theta, is he alright?' asked Jack urgently.

At this Blue went very quiet, she felt in her pocket and held out a small figure about the same size as the figure Jack had found in the attic.

'Is that Theta?' asked Jack with horror. Blue nodded and handed the figure to him. Jack took Theta and looked at him intently, 'We are going to get you back to proper size. I promise you,' he told the little figure intently. At that he felt a slight but sudden warmth in his hand. 'He's still alive,' pronounced Jack.

'How do you know, Jack?' asked Twiggy who had just walked in.

'I just do,' said Jack firmly.

Nick walked into the cave. Without greeting Jack, he started glumly, 'I have bad news, we can't go back the way we came. Apparently, people who have tried to go into The Fault from this side just get spat out again. And the only place out of this valley is far up the mountains, with another of those awful holes, and no one who has ever gone into them has come out alive. The people here rarely even go near the entrance as it is such a hard climb. We are completely stuck here forever. Forever in this boring, *boring* village.' As he finished, he kicked at a small rock with his toe and flinched as he found it harder than he'd expected. 'Wake up, wake up, wake up!' he implored himself.

'The people here don't really want us to stay anyway,' said Twiggy. 'They think that horrible people might follow us here, and they don't want trouble. But they told me that they would be happy to provide guides to where they think the hole could be.'
'Is that right?' Blue asked the woman standing quietly to one side

The woman nodded, 'I am sorry but we lead simple lives. The wolves make us nervous. And the leopard makes us even *more* nervous. Since she has been here the yaks are not providing as much milk,' said the woman a little embarrassed.

Blue felt immediately sorry, and suggested that the moment Jack felt better, they would all move on.

She and Twiggy left Jack who was tired, to sleep again. They walked together to the water's edge. The leopard settled on the warm bank, she seemed less fond of the water. But as Blue watched her, she suddenly leapt into the stream and emerged with a large fish in her mouth which she ate delicately. 'As long as she keeps to fish and doesn't move to yak,' worried Blue.

She jumped as the leopard transmitted back to her, 'The yak are far too big, but one of those little goats…'

Blue transmitted urgently back, 'You must promise not to touch any of the animals that are being cared for by these people, or we will have to leave before we are ready.' The big cat looked in her direction with its eyes half closed.

'How did Jack take the news about Theta?' Twiggy asked.

'I gave him to Jack, who is sure that he is still alive, but I don't think he is,' said Blue.

Twiggy frowned, 'I'm finding it difficult to remember what it was like before we met Theta,' she confessed.
This information worried Blue. She too had noticed that she was losing touch with reality. When she thought of never seeing her mother again, she felt a certain pang. When she thought of never seeing the snow leopard again, she felt even worse.

'Twiggy, ask the wolves about The Life Spirit,' urged Blue.

Twiggy transmitted to the wolves. 'They say that they have heard of a Life Spirit and know that it is in the mountains somewhere in another valley. There are snow leopards on the other side too. The wolves are eager to leave in that direction and have invited us to join them. They are finding it difficult to live with so much yak and goat meat available'

'Yes,' agreed Blue, 'the snow leopard is wondering what goat would taste like and the woman says that the yaks are so nervous that they aren't producing as much milk as they should.'

'I wonder if Nick will be up for it?' mused Twiggy, as they all watched Nick walking up the stream towards them.

Surprisingly Nick was very keen to get to The Life Spirit, or anywhere that was not right there. 'All I want is to get back to normal life,' he announced nasally. His nose had not mended properly and was affecting the way he talked. He did not seem to be daunted by the task ahead.

Blue returned to Jack to tell him that when he was better, they would have to leave. She found him with the reindeer and talking to other villagers. When she heard what they were talking about she realised that they were all coming to the same conclusion.

'Some of the younger villagers are going to help us up the first slopes. They have all heard of The Life Spirit and believe that it lives high up in a hidden valley. They will start us in the general direction and the reindeer will pull the sleigh with extra supplies. They will come as far as they dare, before sending us on our way. We can't stay here, the yaks…'

'Aren't milking as well as usual,' said Blue finishing his sentence. 'But are you well enough Jack?'

'I don't know what's in these drinks, but I can just feel them giving me strength.'

Blue gave him a hug but shivered as she saw the extent of the bruising around his wrists and onto his hands.

'Perhaps we should wait until the bruising has gone?' she suggested.

'I'll be fine Blue. If I get tired, I'll take lots of rests in the sleigh,' promised Jack. As the sun fell, bonfires were being lit by the villagers. Delicious smells wafted round their small circular dwellings. As the evening wore on everyone learned that the visitors were leaving. The chief chose three young men and a young female to accompany the visitors. The males were called Pemba, Tenzing and Ang, and the female was Meesha. There was much excitement among the group who had been chosen.

Pemba came up to introduce himself, 'I will take my yak Gentian with me to make sure that you don't go without milk for the first part of your trip,' he assured them.

Misha and Tenzing joined the party. Ang seemed a little shy but stood close by.

Pemba said, 'Ang always yearns for adventure. He is strong and capable and certainly not put on this earth to be a farmer. He'll look after you and bring you back safely.'

Blue replied, 'But we are not coming back, we have to get...' she concentrated for a moment hard, '... yes, we have to get back to our own homes,' she finished triumphantly.

'Oh? Are your homes on the other side of the mountains?' asked Meesha.

'Some mountains, but I don't think these are the ones,' replied Blue miserably.

She saw that Nick was frowning. 'Don't worry Nick' she said.

'Why should I be worried?' asked Nick 'This is just a horrid dream and I *am* going to wake up sometime and thankfully forget all about it,' he announced.

Twiggy felt her aches and pains, she smelt the damp fur of the wolves overlaid with wood smoke and baking bread. She shivered as the sun disappeared behind the mountains. Yak bells rang on the night air as the herd came in to be milked.

'Well, if this is a dream it sounds and smells awfully real to me,' she said. She went to join Jack round the campfire and eat the thick soup proffered to her, which tasted so nourishing.

'How's Nick?' asked Jack.

'He keeps talking about our life before, which he says is real, but when he talks, I find it doesn't seem real to me,' replied Twiggy thoughtfully.

'What stuff, like school and families and…' said Jack trying to concentrate. 'It seems very hazy all of that,' he agreed. 'Isn't it amazing that we can understand these people?'

'And the awful people before,' agreed Blue.

That night all the young slept fitfully.

The next morning, to the sound of music blown through yak horns, the party set off.

They spent the morning walking up the valley beside the merry stream. The gentle reindeer already looked fitter. Their wounds were healing. They were benefiting from the strong grass and varied herbs that grew on the floor of the valley.

At noon they stopped to fish and the snow leopard disappeared to hunt in the rocks above. She brought back a small goat-like creature which she and the wolves devoured at a respectful distance.

'Exactly where are we going?' Jack asked Pemba.

'Between the pass and over that mountain,' he replied. Just as he finished speaking, they heard a dramatic bugling in the sky. A group of large birds were flying above them, their necks stretched out in front and their legs trailing behind.
'Herons!' exclaimed Twiggy.

'No,' corrected Ang. 'They are demoiselles cranes. We see them at this time every year. They migrate over the Himalayas.'

Everyone watched the cranes flying, their calls becoming fainter until they disappeared out of sight.

'That's what you need for where you are going,' said Ang grimly. 'Wings.'

They camped at the head of the valley. It was fascinating watching the villagers setting up the tents. They made a hut shape from wooden poles they had brought, and then covered them with skins. Everyone else gathered flotsam from the side of the stream and added what they found to the sticks they had brought with them. As the sun disappeared people and animals crowded round the fire, and the young were grateful for the thick soup and the tough but tasty bread.

'It's a camping life for me,' hummed Blue as she settled down with the snow leopard curled round her. The rest of the party crept into the hut and it soon became so stuffy that they all dropped off to a deep sleep, waking in the morning with rather thick heads. The clarity of the air outside soon cleared the stuffiness as they ate their modest breakfast.

'The most disgusting I have ever drunk,' was Nick's response to the strong cup of coffee he was given. Twiggy however, was developing a taste for the coffee.

After breakfast, Pemba brought them all furry shoes. On the soles the fur went in different directions.

'These will help you grip the mountain,' nodded Tenzing

'But we can't leave our ski boots behind; they cost so much to rent and we've already lost our skiis!' gasped Blue. Seeing her distress Tenzing assured her that he could carry them in his backpack.

'Perhaps it would be better if we stayed here forever,' suggested Twiggy, as she cupped her hands round the wooden bowl, the steam wreathing out from the scalding black liquid.

Hearing this, Tenzing and Pemba gave her beaming smiles, 'No one could be more welcome, we believe it is you who will bring back our bees to the valley,' they said in unison bowing their heads.

'Where have your bees gone?' asked Twiggy. But there was no time for explanations.

'Time to move out!' called Ang. Blue helped Meesha hitch the reindeer to the sleigh. Nothing was wasted, even burnt bits of wood were stored carefully in the sleigh.

Each day passed similarly. They wound their way up faint paths, entering a world that became snowier as they got higher. They saw wild goats and antelope, who stared at them curiously. The most curious paid with their lives. Sometimes the wolves or mostly the leopard would bring one down. As food became scarcer, the Mountain People and the children became grateful for the occasional meal with meat. But the reindeer would look glum, and they shifted their feet and pawed the snow nervously when they smelt the meat cooking or heard the wolves hunting.

Twiggy scratched them with a fork-shaped stick. 'We will never eat you, I promise,' she whispered into their ears.

Each day became a little harder, there was less food and the way became steeper. A cold wind picked up and nipped at their ears and noses. Nick was glad of his gloves given to him by the Mountain People. He thought longingly of the time when he had taken off his own gloves and wondered if they were still sitting in the snow. He wondered if his parents were alright and if they were searching for him. A tear slipped down his cheek.

When the party found a way that was sheltered from the wind, they found that the snow was deep and soft and it was almost impossible for the humans to make a way, so they were forced to choose a path between the most sheltered and the most exposed. They used their own experience to choose the right way, but also kept half an eye on the snow leopard because they trusted her to keep Blue out of danger. The leopard was aloof to the others. It was only against Blue that she rubbed her great head and purred under Blue's caresses.

Jack's companion was his board - his Avalanche Rider. As he carried it strapped to his back, he could hear it humming encouragingly to him. It was impossible to take lifts in the sleigh any longer. One day the moment came when it was clearly too steep, and the way too narrow, for the sleigh to travel further.

The Pemba unpacked the last portions of food, and hid some under rocks for their return journey. They unharnessed the reindeer to let them run free. Then they shared out supplies into backpacks for everyone.

'Mine's heavier than Jack's,' grumbled Nick testing his against Jack's.

Jack arriving to pick up his pack said, 'Take mine instead Nick, I'll carry yours, I don't mind.' He felt so strong and was exhilarated by the exercise. At that moment he was not daunted by the dramatic mountains looming over them.

Ang looked at Nick thoughtfully. 'We have estimated the food needs of each individual and it is advisable to carry your own rations, in your own pack.'

Nick suddenly realised that if his pack was heavier, it might mean it contained more food. He snatched it up and marched on.

'Well, that sorted that out,' laughed Twiggy. She smiled at Jack, and he noticed that her eyes were exactly the colour of the lake that they could see below them.

'Does that lake have a name?' he asked Ang.

'No, it's just a lake,' answered Ang.

'I'm going to call it Twiggy Lake, because it is the same colour as Twiggy's eyes,' said Jack. Twiggy blushed and Blue nudged Twiggy as they walked off again. Jack blushed too. Whatever had come over him? he wondered. He blushed again when the heard the girls laughing together; he was sure that they were laughing at him. He had read somewhere that you could become quite lightheaded at altitude. He hoped that he was not getting altitude sickness. He wondered if Nick had overheard, but Nick seemed to be in his own world.

'I don't know whether I prefer going up or coming down,' Nick grumbled. His nose was still swollen and although his eyes were open, they were rimmed with bruising.

Jack felt sorry for him. 'Don't worry, just look at the view and think of what an adventure we're having,' he said cheerily. 'The sun is going down fast. We'll soon be making camp and it's going to be a fantastic sunset.'

A little further on, Jack nearly stepped on a hare. It had sat still trying to remain invisible. But at the last second it leapt away and dropped swiftly down the mountain. Jack was suddenly reminded of his dog Ruff. Ruff would have found that white bobbing tail irresistible. Jack looked over his shoulder hoping that the wolves and the leopard were not close, but then he heard the wolves hunting something much further below. He could not see any sign of the leopard. The path, such as it was, twisted and turned so at any one time the view behind and in front was obscured by the bluffs and frozen outcrops. He guessed the leopard would be striding close to Blue and felt briefly envious of their friendship. He reached with his hand for Avalanche Rider, and it hummed lightly back to him.

'We make camp here!' called out Ang some way above him. And five minutes later Jack had joined him. Above him the sky looked almost turquoise. There were wisps of clouds, their edges smudged with crimson and flame. Immediately Jack forgot about his home and Ruff. He stood still celebrating the view. He felt nowhere else in the world could make him feel so alive and so much part of the earth. The temperature was dropping as quickly as the sun, and he shivered. Only then did Jack move gratefully towards a crackling fire.

But he did not spend long beside the fire. Meesha called him over and showed him how to set up the tents. He pulled animal skins over short light poles. He soon got warm collecting rocks to weigh the skins down.

'The test of a well-prepared tent is when it's still standing after a mountain storm,' said Meesha.

By now the others had joined them and it was quite dark. On the outer edge of the fire, he could see the wolves settling down for the night. The leopard stalked round onto the opposite side.

The young and the Mountain People made a circle round the fire and Tenzing gave them a hot herbal drink. In the middle of the fire was a terracotta pot and inside the pot Tenzing had put a sort of dough to cook into bread. He was slicing dried meat and apricots to make a stew. 'Nick has kneaded the dough and we are baking bread everyone!' he called out in his cheerful voice.

Now Nick had a pestle and mortar and was crushing herbs. Blue thought that it was the first time she had ever seen him look happy.

Blue asked Meesha about life in the mountains and how they lived with the cold. Meesha replied that there was an abundance of food in the summer and that when the land froze, they ate what they had dried from the summer's harvest.

Jack remembered how Theta had warmed the stones and he asked Meesha if she could warm stones too. She listened to his story intently but shook her head.

'There are a people who have that gift,' she told Jack 'But what happened to the person you speak of?'

At that point Jack realised that he would have to tell Meesha about Theta, and he pulled Theta from his pocket. To his delight he could see that Theta was bigger.

Meesha looked at Theta with an expression approaching horror, she called urgently to Ang, Pemba and Tenzing.

'What do you hold here?' asked Pemba.

Blue who had joined them, said hurriedly 'Theta is good, he saved us from the Ravening Wolves, he led us through The Fault, but he lost energy somehow and has become very small. Oh!' she exclaimed pleased as she looked at Theta, 'he's bigger!'

'We must hear all your story,' said Tenzing 'So we can understand this figure.'

The fire was dying before the young had finished telling the villagers all that had gone on before.

The villagers were silent, but they looked at each other with glances and nods. The young were sure that they were communicating silently to each other.

At last Pemba spoke, 'We can give Theta some strength, but not tonight we are too tired. At dawn tomorrow when we are rested, we will come together to help restore him.'

This was hopeful news for the young and they slept more soundly than the night before. They all awoke a little before dawn. Tenzing was relighting the fire. Jack could see that Nick was already helping Ang get some sort of breakfast together.

Pemba came over to Jack and asked him to bring the figure of Theta to where Tenzing and Meesha were sitting facing each other.

Jack reached for Theta and to his delight found that Theta was bigger than the night before. He pointed this out to Pemba who nodded. 'It's something in the air, or perhaps the ancient rocks are restoring him,' he mused.

Theta was placed on a mat between Tenzing and Meesha. Meesha offered him what looked like a small, amber-coloured pill, but Theta seemed unable to react.

Then Meesha looked intently at Tenzing, who leant over Theta and held her hands. They started to chant softly to each other. Jack could hear his snowboard Avalanche Rider humming too. The wolves whined tentatively. The leopard sat up expectantly. Meesha and Tenzing concentrated on each other a little more and they looked into each other's eyes. Suddenly they stopped chanting and the wolves went silent. Meesha and Tenzing nodded and dropped each other's hands.

Beneath them was a movement, and the small figure was now the size of a large dog. It sat up.
'Theta!' cried Blue delightedly.

Theta shook his head, 'I'm afraid I'm not myself,' he said dazedly. He looked about himself. He seemed to understand the situation when he said, 'I will do my best to accompany you, and well done all of you for coming so far!'

'Can't you make him his normal size?' asked Twiggy. But even as she asked, she could see the answer. Both Tenzing and Meesha looked strained, and Pemba was pressing porridge on them to give them back their strength.

'We wanted to give him one of our precious Life Spirit bee pills, but he says that they do him more harm than good, very rarely there are some who can have a bad reaction,' said Meesha sadly, 'and it seems that Theta is one of those.'

Theta nodded, 'But I have a feeling that we are travelling in the right direction. I just hope I don't hold you up, you intrepid travellers you! Thank you, young Nick,' he said, as he accepted porridge from Nick, 'I see you carry war wounds?'

'They're not really real though they hurt,' said Nick, 'I am just playing along in this nightmare.'

'What is this *nightmare*, you keep talking about?' asked Ang. 'Is the heat of this fire not real? Put your hand in it to find out. Is that rock not real? Press your lips against it; feel how cold it is. Smell the herbs that you are crushing?' He sounded hurt and angry. Nick looked embarrassed.

'Ang, I know that everything around us feels awfully real, and that you and your friends are doing everything to help us, but I want to go home. I want to know how my father is; he was ill just before we went into that horrible tunnel. He may even be dead!' At that, two large tears rolled down Nick's cheeks. Meesha immediately got up and patted him on the back. She gave him a hot drink and spoke to him in a low voice. She kept repeating what she said, it sounded as though she was chanting again. Blue was so mesmerised that she forgot to drink her tea and when she next took a sip it was cold.

Twiggy, Blue and Jack looked at each other, they tried to remember Nick's father, but it was impossible. Worse still, every time that Twiggy got a picture in her mind of her mother it faded away and, instead, she was distracted by the smell of herbs coming from the tea she was drinking.

That day of climbing was much harder. Despite his protests Theta often had to be carried.

It was a despondent group that made camp that night.

Realising that everyone was low the villagers got some musical instruments from their packs and started to sing softly. Twiggy gave herself up to the music and stopped trying to search through her mind for things that seemed too unreal and too difficult to fathom.

That night it was much colder and in the middle of the night, when they had all gone to sleep the wolves woke up and howled at the moon. Everyone listened especially Twiggy who understood their cries. They cried into the great night sky a story, describing their lost hunting grounds and their fears of men with guns. She could not say when they finished their lament. But she must have gone back to sleep again, because when she next woke it was dawn, and she heard again the calling of demoiselle cranes above.

She climbed out from under the furry skins to stand outside the tent, where Jack was already up and staring into the sky.

'I wonder what they are saying to each other?' mused Jack as he looked after the silhouettes of the birds disappearing into the distance.

'Yes, I wonder too,' Twiggy replied. 'The ones we saw a few days ago sounded hopeful; these sound rather frantic.'

Tenzing, who was bringing Twiggy a mug of tea, nodded. 'You are right I can see a young one who is lagging behind, and they are trying to encourage him to keep up. They have to get over the Himalayas before the storms, or they are doomed.'

'Oh dear, what will happen if the young one is too tired?' asked Twiggy.

'They'll be forced to leave it behind and if we are lucky, we'll find it on our way and it will go in our pot,' replied Tenzing matter of factly.

'I couldn't eat it!' answered Twiggy.

'Well, if you were that hungry and it was going to be wasted, you too would be pleased to make some use of the carcass. Ignoring good protein up high in the mountains is a luxury we cannot afford,' said Ang agreeing with Tenzing.

'Where are we going today?' asked Jack changing the subject. He could see that Twiggy's thoughts were on the young demoiselle crane and she looked entirely crestfallen.

They all looked at the way ahead, where the great wall of the first mountain loomed. Blue emerged from a hole which had been dug by the leopard who followed her out and they both stretched and yawned.

'Where are we going today?' Jack repeated to Tenzing.

'Today we will do some real climbing and tomorrow, or the next day, we will find out if it is true as our ancestors tell us in song, whether there is a way through the mountain,' he sounded excited. 'From now on this is all new to me and today we leave the yak and reindeer behind, so eat a good breakfast, tomorrow it will be short rations!'

'What was that about short rations?' asked Nick suspiciously, emerging from his tent.

'We've got some climbing to do, and we leave the yak and reindeer behind', explained Jack.

'I'm not sure that I'm a climber; I'll stay with the reindeer,' volunteered Nick.

'Then you'll go hungry,' laughed Meesha who overheard. 'We are taking all the food. And the reindeer and yak will be eating mostly moss and lichens until they find their way back to our village.'

Nick winced, he looked at the mountain face rising in front of him. He looked back at everyone else and all he could mutter was, 'What a total nightmare.'

Chapter 15

For three days they climbed. The Mountain Men were quick and sure-footed. The children did their best, but as soon as they had to climb up nearly sheer places, Twiggy discovered that she suffered from vertigo. Even when she was roped and was held above by Meesha, she still froze. On several occasions Ang had to climb down to her and move her hands and feet to get her started again.

Blue and Jack managed well, and to his surprise, Nick found a rhythm and began to enjoy the process. On two occasions Ang let him feed the rope to Blue. Pemba and Ang were the path finders and they were always way in front. Sometimes the track split and they would leave a message chipped in ice to indicate the best route. Meesha led the children with Nick first, Jack second, then Twiggy and lastly Blue. Tenzing brought up the rear with Theta.

Every stop was most welcome; they all admired the views except Twiggy who was angry with herself for slowing them all up. She sat in a huddle resolutely ignoring everyone else.

The first night they found a reasonably sheltered flat space. They had to make small individual tents. It was much colder. Twiggy snuggled in with the wolves and Blue was as usual being hugged by the leopard. The rest had to rely on only themselves and when they woke at dawn even the villagers moved slower than usual.

Now the mountain reared up in front of them as if to say 'enough'. It looked very forbidding. As they pulled on their packs everyone was quiet except for Ang, who was clearly relishing the challenge. He whistled softly and cheerfully to himself.

As soon as they moved off the small flat camping space, they felt the force of the wind and on the wind were small flurries of snow. Twiggy's face looked dark, and Jack stopped beside her to encourage her.

'Just follow exactly what I do Twiggy, OK?' he said.

'I know what I should do, but I get a feeling that I must jump off the mountain. I feel the void is calling to me,' she said, her jaw straining with tension and a terrible anguish in her voice.

Jack went to tell Meesha how Twiggy was feeling and Meesha called to Tenzing. They puzzled together and then came and circled Twiggy.

'We have a tiny amount of precious bee jewel. It comes from bees only found in our valley, it is very powerful. We have decided to give Twiggy some *and* we can add our hum to make it stronger.'

They gave Twiggy something that looked like a pill; it was green but there were glints of gold in it. It reminded Jack of the lights in The Fault. After Twiggy had swallowed it Meesha and Tenzing put their hands on Twiggy's head and they hummed an incantation. Avalanche Rider joined in, thrumming softly tied to Jack's backpack.

'How do you feel now?' asked Meesha tenderly.

The change in Twiggy was dramatic. 'Awesome!' she replied brightly. 'I can't wait to get going; it's going to be a breeze. Come on everybody,' she called excitedly, 'No time to waste!' Twiggy leapt at the rock face and started scaling up it. Like a monkey she moved lithely up the side.

Nick and Jack looked at each other in amazement.

'Wow!' exclaimed Nick 'Perhaps you would like to hum to all of us Tenzing?'

But Tenzing and Meesha were looking worriedly at Twiggy.

'She is going too fast; perhaps we have given her too much courage,' warned Meesha.

Blue opened her mouth to yell a warning to Twiggy. Immediately Meesha leapt at her and put her hand over Blue's mouth.

'Wha-?' began Blue.

'Do not shout out or you could break the enchantment and she could fall straight off the mountain,' hissed Tenzing to the stunned children.

'Will she be alright?' asked Blue anxiously.

'She will catch up Ang, and if he does not stop her, then Pemba will, I hope,' said Meesha dryly. 'In the meantime, we will observe best climbing practice.' Then she explained again how to use the climbing ropes and what to do if someone falls. They all listened carefully and began their ascent. After several hours toiling with many stops to catch their breath, they caught up with Pemba, who was melting snow to make a herbal tea. 'Where's Twiggy?' asked Jack.

'She's had a drink and something to eat and is going on to catch up Ang. She's quite a climber your friend, I hadn't noticed,' he said with admiration in his voice.

'Yesterday she was terrified', replied Jack shortly. 'Meesha and Tenzing sang into her mind and she stopped being frightened,' he explained, as he looked up the steep mountain face in front of him. 'How did she get up that?' he gasped.

'Like a cat,' answered Pemba.

Meesha's face appeared over the edge, and she climbed onto the plateau.

'How long will the enchantment last?' Pemba asked.

Meesha shook her head, 'We thought we needed to put a strong spell on her as she was terrified of the heights, but she is incredibly suggestible. She became as brave as a lion and I have never seen someone react so strongly. Pemba, she was up the mountain before we had a chance to stop her, and we dared not call out because that might've cancelled the spell and I daresay that she would fall straight off the side. She could be in terrible danger.'

'Will Ang stop her?' asked Jack.

'Not necessarily. He will assume that she's got over her fears and is a brilliant climber,' said Pemba. 'Indeed, she is a brilliant climber!'

'Can't we call ahead to Ang?' asked Blue urgently and then stopped as she realised that she already knew the answer. A soft head pressed against her shoulder and whiskers tickled her under her chin. It was the snow leopard, who usually climbed alone, but now joined them on the ledge. Suddenly Blue had an idea.

'Please help snow leopard,' she transmitted to the big cat and explained what had happened to Twiggy. Immediately the big cat leapt gracefully away.

'What's happening?' asked Meesha.

'She's going to see what she can do,' answered Blue.

'Do you mean that the leopard actually understands you?' asked Tenzing sharply. 'Are you a witch?'

'Yes… No,' stuttered Blue. 'Yes, the leopard seems to understand me, but I'm not a witch, witches don't exist,' she finished.

There was a small silence. Tenzing and Meesha exchanged glances and looked uncomfortable.

'The leopard helped us escape from that horrible village we told you about,' said Blue trying to reassure the Tenzing and Meesha.

Although Tenzing nodded thoughtfully the atmosphere had changed, it was not so easy and none of the children could really understand why.

'In this land,' suggested Nick under his breath, 'where snowboards, wolves and leopards communicate with humans, I should imagine witches *do* exist,' he said sarcastically.

'Well, you know I'm not one!' snapped back Blue.

They climbed on steadily through the afternoon and although they worried about Twiggy, most of the time they had to concentrate solely on the climbing. Tenzing patiently hammered in iron footholds or chipped away at the rock to make handholds. This made the way easier for all of them.

After a particularly steep place, Tenzing and Meesha rewarded them with boiled sweets made from honey.

'These are wonderful!' gasped Blue feeling the sweet energy coursing through her veins.

Meesha smiled. She seemed to have recovered from learning that Blue could communicate with the leopard. 'These sweets are made from the snow bees and they have magical properties. They will replenish your energy. They're not nearly as strong as the bee jewel I gave Twiggy,' she reassured them looking embarrassed. 'Unfortunately, we can only use them sparingly as snow bees are very rare and I only have a few sweets and a tiny piece of bee jewel.'

Nick smiled happily as he sucked on his. In the cold temperatures the swelling on his face had subsided and he had lost weight. He looked a great deal happier and fitter.

'When I get back to normal life, I'm going to take up mountaineering,' he said.

'Not too many mountains in Norfolk,' pointed out Blue.

'But you can join clubs and things. I'd like to do that too,' said Jack. Suddenly he had a strong memory of his school and home; it came out of the blue and gave him a most extraordinary feeling.

'We could join together,' said Nick companionably.

'Yes! that would be fun,' agreed Jack, much to his surprise.

There was a soft call from up above. Tenzing and Meesha had been making a way through a split in a rock above them, it had looked very hazardous, and they had moved slowly. But now they were inviting the children to climb up the foot and handholds that they had made for them.

They caught up with Twiggy as daylight was failing. She was about to leave to 'finish the climb' as she put it but the 'beastly leopard won't let go of me.'

Ang was watching concernedly.

Twiggy took a lot of persuading but eventually she calmed down and Meesha quickly made a sleep-inducing potion. It was a worried and uncomfortable group that settled down to sleep that night. The ledge was narrow and all of them had nightmares about falling off it.

They awoke at dawn stiff and cold. It was only Twiggy who was able to bustle about cheerfully. She was helping Pemba make tea and anxious to get everyone going again. The leopard trotted about close to her.

'Hurry up, I think the wolves have found the entrance to the way through the mountains. We have a few hours of stiff climbing and then we will be there!' she announced excitedly to everyone.

'The wolves?' questioned Ang, 'The wolves have long since gone. They will go round the mountains, not up them.' He shook his head at Twiggy as though he thought she had completely lost her mind.

Twiggy either did not hear what he said or could not be bothered to reply. 'Blue, can you stop this dratted leopard from following me around?'

Blue looked hurt at the snow leopard being described as 'dratted' but she kept her feelings to herself.

'She's just keeping an eye on you so that when you are climbing really fast, she can stop you from falling,' explained Blue.

'I absolutely guarantee that I won't fall. What a ridiculous idea! Pemba did I look as if I was in any danger of falling?' appealed Twiggy to Pemba.

Pemba shook his head. 'Twiggy, climbing in the mountains is a team activity, the mountain will pick us off one by one, unless we act together. You are a gifted climber but just a tiny slip and there is no second chance on the icy face, so it's best that you buddy up with the snow leopard, as you refuse to wait for the rest of us,' he said dryly.

But Twiggy was not even slightly abashed. In fact, she seemed more confident than ever.

'Meesha when is the potion going to wear off?' asked Jack.

'Perhaps when she has a shock, perhaps never; I can't tell,' admitted Meesha.

Nick came to stand next to Jack. 'What we need to do is to find what The Life Spirit is, and with any luck it will show us how to end this nightmare and make things normal.'

Jack no longer knew what normal was, but he did feel an irresistible pull to continue up the mountain and find The Life Spirit.

They finished their hard oat biscuits and were allowed one marvellous honey sweet. The moment the sweet touched their tongues, the rest of their bodies responded with delight. It was as if their blood ran stronger and the aches and pains disappeared. Instead of feeling cold and despondent, each one felt optimistic and enthusiastic about the climb.

They loaded their makeshift tents onto their backs and attacked the mountain. It was even more technical than the day before, but now they were all efficient in the use of the yak hair ropes.

Blue watched in admiration as Jack chipped out neat footholds and handholds in the rock and the ice. *We have all become mountaineers,* she marvelled to herself.

Meesha, Tenzing and Blue were nominated as the first team. Behind them came the next group; Nick, Jack, Pemba and Ang with Theta bringing up the rear.

Twiggy and the snow leopard had left earlier. Blue was not sure if Twiggy had even eaten anything.

'You will leave some signs and call to us occasionally to let us know that you're alright?' she'd asked as Twiggy had started to scale the rock face.

'Yes of course I will!' Twiggy had called over her left shoulder as she'd nonchalantly clung to the side with a few fingers and not much more than her big toe in a crevice.

'I can't bear to look!' Blue had shaken her head.

'Nor me,' Jack had shuddered, nevertheless his eyes had been glued to Twiggy's fast-disappearing figure.

That had been earlier in the morning and now it was the rest of the team's turn to face the mountain climb again.

'Jack when we get to The Life Spirit, what exactly are we going to do?' asked Blue.

'I don't know,' answered Jack. 'I just know that I'm with Avalanche Rider, and Avalanche Rider wants me to go in a certain direction, and until Avalanche Rider stops somehow driving me, then I can't stop,' he said simply. He searched Blue's face hoping that she understood.

'What are you waiting for?' called Nick. He was already paying out the rope, he looked efficient and in control. His face glowed healthily and there was only some mild yellowing and a tinge of blue where he had been hit with Dame Malintention's vicious stick.

'Come on,' said Blue, briefly hugging Jack. 'Perhaps today everything will be sorted out.'
But after an hour, things changed and they felt less confident. The climb was very steep. Everyone strained muscles and stretched to find footholds. Those that were roped were so grateful that others had found the path before them.

Once, Jack nearly came off the mountain; one arm and leg swung wildly, and his back and Avalanche Rider clashed against a rock. Avalanche Rider hummed and thrummed a high concerned note, chiming in with Jack's dismayed yell. Meesha who was paying out the rope round Jack was well braced and called down to him that he was alright. Blue and Nick looked on, worry creasing their faces.

Eventually Jack joined the others on the tiny ledge and they set off again. Panting and gasping in the thin air, Jack felt that there was not a muscle in his body that was not stretched to its limit. They inched their way up a great crack bracing against the two walls. Climbing within the scar took them out of the unrelenting wind. Momentarily, it was wonderful to be out of the extreme cold, but then they felt the force of the sun hitting their backs.

'Well, I may have been complaining about being cold this morning,' panted Nick, 'Now I'm absolutely drenched with sweat.' His cheeks were bright red and his eyes showed the strain he was under.

'Keep climbing!' urged Tenzing from above.

'Yessir!' replied Nick, his eyes rolling back into his head as he looked at Jack and Blue.

'He's worried that we may have to spend another night on the mountain,' explained Blue intuitively, 'The supplies are pretty low.'

'Well, I don't mind, less to carry,' said Nick. 'I wish we could have more of those amazing sweets. I'm going to get the recipe,' he said enthusiastically. 'I'll make a fortune if I sold those at home.'

The thought of the honey sweets helped them climb again. Jack felt he could hear the bees buzzing. He had such a strong sensation of being a bee that he wondered if he could fly.

Then he heard Blue scream...

'Watch out!' exclaimed Tenzing sharply as he caught Jack under his armpit and hauled him onto another ledge. 'What do you think you were doing? Why did you let go?' he demanded, looking shocked.

'I thought of the honey sweet and then I was sure I could fly,' muttered Jack feeling rather faint. He could feel his heart galloping under his ribs.

'No more sweets for you, I'm afraid. You are a strange people; it seems our medicines are too strong for you, yet you have travelled where we have not dared and come from a place which we do not know how to reach. You are both stronger and weaker than us.' He shook his head in wonder. He rubbed Jack's shoulders hard. 'Now what are you thinking?'

'That I'm pretty tired and you have very strong hands, ouch!' replied Jack.

'That's better!' nodded Tenzing.

They made their way up another section of the mountain face. Now they could dimly hear a howling. Everyone looked at each other.

'The wolves!' gasped Meesha.

'How have they possibly got above us?' asked Pemba.

'They must have gone many times the distance that we have taken,' answered Ang, frowning thoughtfully, who had just climbed up to join Blue. 'They will have quested many routes and taken big risks and probably climbed many false ways and then had to retrace their tracks. I too am surprised they are still travelling with us, I thought they would travel the valleys, and go around the mountains, even if it took many years to find their homes.'

'I hate it when they howl like that,' said Blue, 'They sound so sad.'

'As if they are in mourning,' agreed Nick.

'But they're not moving, they've stopped,' said Jack listening carefully. 'Do you think they have found the way through the mountains?'

They all listened intently.

Ang stood up. 'I think we can reach them before nightfall if we keep going. Come on everyone, one last effort…'

Chapter 16

Night fell before they could reach the wolves and they had not caught up with Twiggy or the snow leopard either.

'I hope she's alright,' worried Blue. She snuggled up with Jack. Jack felt relieved that the leopard was not with them, as the night was bitter and he needed someone to get really close to. Theta and the villagers who were hairy and tougher than the children, encircled them. In the night there was a light snowstorm and the snow built up a layer over the skins that covered them. Only then did they feel a little warmer and at last they could fall into a light sleep for an hour or two.

At dawn they ate the last portion of oat cakes. If the children could not negotiate The Fault in the rock they would have to return. Meesha was constantly working out how much food they could allow themselves. She chipped a honey sweet into tiny shards to give to the children.

'The last whole one is for Twiggy,' she said in a low voice.

Even Nick knew that this was fair. He shuddered to think of the toll that Twiggy had put on herself to be so much further up the mountain.

Even though the golden honey shards were slim, they nevertheless gave them the energy to roll their skins and heave on their backpacks.

Theta, who seemed to be gaining strength and size the further up the mountain they went, started climbing with Tenzing, inching their way up a crevice towards the place where they had heard the wolves.

'Do you want me to help you carry your Avalanche Rider?' asked Pemba to Jack.

'There's no need thank you,' said Jack, 'Avalanche Rider is as light as a feather.'

'This is no time for heroics,' said Ang sharply. 'Pemba will carry the board You nearly fell yesterday, Jack,' he pointed out.

Reluctantly Jack untied Avalanche Rider and handed the board to Pemba who reached out for it. As Pemba took Avalanche Rider in his arms he staggered with the weight and cried out in alarm. Tenzing had to steady him and Meesha leapt up in horror, as both males teetered on the edge. Avalanche Rider vibrated, creating a high whine, not of anger but of concern. Above them the wolves started howling again.

'Take it back!' exclaimed Pemba unnecessarily as Jack was already reaching for Avalanche Rider and the snowboard was moving towards his hand. Jack re-tied the snowboard to his backpack and swung the load effortlessly onto his shoulders.

The Pemba and Ang exchanged glances, and Ang bowed his head briefly towards Jack, 'I'm sorry Jack, I was wrong to act so tactlessly.'

'No, no, don't say sorry, you were trying to be kind,' said Jack a bit breathlessly. 'It's just we seem bound to each other...' he finished, looking at his board.

They became silent as they sorted out the ropes and began to follow the route that Theta and mostly Tenzing were making for them.

They had not climbed far when they were faced with a massive frozen waterfall, barring their way to a steep face the other side. Luckily the steep face had a clear diagonal crack across it and would be easy to climb.

Chipped in the ice were the words *Twiggy woz here!* and an arrow pointed across the waterfall. Beside the waterfall there were long nail scratches, where the leopard had clearly fought for a hold.

Blue's eyes filled with tears as she could read the awful struggle that had taken place. She searched anxiously for signs on the other side, to show her that the leopard was safe. Two wolves suddenly peeped over the edge of the waterfall: one was Illanna and the other Ataaki. Blue wondered where the rest of the pack was.

Half an hour later, after chipping footholds in the ice waterfall, the rest of the party arrived on a large flat ledge. Beyond them was a cave. Warm air was coming out of it and there were yellow-flowered shrubs growing out of a crack in the rocks. On the ledge were several figures, one was Twiggy lying there not moving and the other ones were the mother demoiselle crane and her young son whom they had seen flying in the sky before. Behind Twiggy on the other side were Illanna, Ataaki and another two wolves. The young crane was lying exhausted, with his head under his wing.

Blue and Jack ran forward. The mother demoiselle crane hopped and flapped back a couple of spindly steps.

'Don't frighten her!' called out Twiggy, rallying. Blue and Jack moved more carefully towards the group.

'This young crane is exhausted,' she panted, 'and the wolves want to eat him, and they have lost one of their friends who fell down a ravine. I don't even know where the leopard is; she went down the tunnel hours ago, and I'm so tired I can't move either,' she gasped, lay down and closed her eyes.

'Meesha has one last honey sweet, she'll be here in seconds, hang on Twiggy,' urged Jack.

Theta sat beside her and tried to transmit warmth into her. It must have a worked a little as Twiggy whispered, 'Thank you Theta.'

But Theta shook his head. 'I'm still so weak,' he muttered hopelessly.

Meesha's head popped up from behind the ledge and Nick pulled her onto the flat surface. She quickly opened her backpack and found the precious last snow honey sweet and rushed forward to hand it to Twiggy. Twiggy took it and looked at it for a moment and, before anyone could stop her, she popped it into the young crane's beak. The crane looked momentarily surprised, then it gulped and swallowed the sweet.

'Twiggy!' cried Meesha in horror.

The young crane raised its head, straightened its neck and in one rush it ran for the ledge, followed swiftly by its mother and the hungry she-wolves who could see their meal, disappearing.

Too late the cranes dropped below their sight; the wolves skidded to a halt and looked down disappointed. Moments later the cranes swooped into sight. They flew low over the party; their cries of delight and excitement made Blue cry out, 'Good luck, good luck!'

Everyone could see what a difference the snow honeybee sweet had made. The two great birds flew straight up into the sky, the young one easily leading its mother.

They watched as the specks grew smaller and smaller.

'Those sweets,' stated Nick, 'are just awesome.'

'Wow Twiggy,' said Jack 'you saved that bird.' But Twiggy did not answer, deathly pale she lay stretched out. Pemba dropped by her side and took her pulse.

'It's very faint,' he said.

Meesha searched through her snow honeybee purse for the merest fragment that she could dilute with snow, but there was nothing.

Ang said to Jack, 'Come on, we must explore the cave.'

Jack dashed off with him to see what they could find. Not far inside the cave was a drop off with chaotic swirling lights, much like the great abyss they had jumped into before. The leopard was pacing backwards and forwards as if willing herself to jump. She gave a welcoming moan to Jack when she saw him and pawed at the edge of the huge hole.

'No future here,' said Ang grimly.

'You're wrong Ang, listen to Avalanche Rider,' replied Jack excitedly. Indeed Avalanche Rider was humming and vibrating on Jack's back. Jack did not dare go too close to the drop off in case Avalanche Rider took him over the edge before the rest of them joined him.

'Get the others quick, we're going to jump into it,' ordered Jack.

'Never!' replied Ang shocked.

'Just get the others quick before Twiggy dies. Go on Ang' repeated Jack.

But just then the rest of the party arrived. Twiggy was draped over Ataaki's back.

'We're going over!' announced Jack. He looked for Theta to support him, and Theta came quickly to his side, holding Blue's hand.

'Never, this is suicide,' shouted Pemba above the roar of the abyss. 'You cannot go over, it is against our laws.' He strode to the edge of the abyss and looked into it, his face contorted with horror. Pemba repeated, 'We will not let you jump here. It is madness and certain death. We will take our chances and return. These are my orders.'

Behind him Jack saw the leopard had curled her tail around Blue's waist. Nick stood on her other side, also holding Theta.

'Come away from the edge!' called Meesha, drawing Tenzing with her to stop anyone from jumping. But even as she warned them, she looked with fascination at the sight before her.

'We've done this before, we told you all!' called out Blue. 'It's our only hope. You must go back to your village. Thank you for all you have done!' Theta spoke above the roaring of the chasm, to Pemba, Ang, Tenzing and Meesha.

Pemba shook his head in disbelief, but suddenly Tenzing spoke urgently to Meesha and they held hands and stepped forward.

'We are coming too!' they shouted.

'I can't hold on for much longer!' yelled Jack, as Avalanche Rider vibrated in his arms.

'Go!' commanded Theta, reaching for Meesha who was holding Ang.

'Have you got Twiggy?' yelled Jack as he and Avalanche Rider stepped over the edge.

'Ataaki's got her and...' shouted Blue as she was already falling into the void, '... I've got Ataaki ... and you,' she said faintly as the wind rushed past her and weird coloured shapes passed her eyes. Her fingers clutched to Jack's backpack and her other hand full of the tough hair belonging to Ataaki. What was most comforting was that she had a tight belt round her waist which she knew was the leopard's tail.

In the background she heard desperate cries of 'Good Luck!' from Pemba.

Jack could hold on. He had pressed Avalanche Rider to the length of his body and instead of holding on to the end corners as he had the last time he had ridden through the earth's faults, *this* time his hands were curled round the front, and he was braced against the board. He was enjoying the experience of flying down tunnels of extraordinary colour, twisting and turning. It seemed to him that Avalanche Rider wanted to follow the blue green paths and to veer violently away from the red, or orange, or purple tunnels that were offered to them at intersections.

As before, the journey through the dark space went on for what seemed a very long time. In fact, Jack was sure that for part of it he lost consciousness, for he dreamt that he and Avalanche Rider were one and he no longer needed to hold on to the Board's top edge. Indeed, he felt confident enough to look back to see how the others were getting on.

Blue and Nick had their eyes tightly shut and the wind pulled at their hair and the skin on their faces. The leopard however looked keen and although her eyes were screwed up, Jack could see the gold glints behind them. There seemed to be three wolves, all with a mouthful of Theta's coat in their jaws. Jack had time to wonder about the other wolves. Perhaps they had taken the long route, the one that Theta had surmised would take them years to reach their destination, wherever that might be.

Just behind him were Meesha and Tenzing. Tenzing had managed to put his arm around Meesha and both looked terrified. Even though Meesha's eyes were tightly closed, Jack could see tears slipping past her temples and her expression conveyed sheer horror. Bravely Tenzing was forcing himself to look ahead, so that if he had the chance, he could protect Meesha for he intended to make her his wife. For a brief moment their eyes met and Jack thought he saw a faint relaxation of Tenzing's features.

The only really worrying sight was Twiggy; she was slumped over the top of Ataaki and appeared completely oblivious to what was going on.

Jack looked back just in time to steer into the blueish green tunnel narrowly missing one that was full of purple light.

'I wonder where that one goes?' he thought fascinated by the possibilities. He began to enjoy the ride and as his pleasure grew so did the speed. He was almost disappointed when the end of the tunnel came into sight and without ceremony, they were all shot into a wall of soft snow.

For a moment they lay there, stunned. From the tunnel came a pleasant blast of warm air. A mountain hare, nibbling the flowers that grew straight from the rock, looked at them with surprise and then scented the wolves and leopard, and hopped away over a ridge. But suddenly it came back looking alarmed. Changing direction altogether, it fled up the mountain side. A moment later Jack could see why: a pair of ears appeared and two magnificent leopards emerged from below. They stopped as they spotted the chaotic sight spread below them. Blue listened to them talking to each other.

'Can this be the right place that The Life Spirit directed us to?' asked one.

'Who are these people?' added the other.

'Snow leopard, snow leopard,' transmitted Blue excitedly, 'look there are two more of your kind!' but she could see no sign of the snow leopard except for a large indentation in the snow beside her. There was a flurry of movement and 'her' snow leopard emerged from the mound, sneezing snow from her nose and shaking her head.

The two arrivals looked on in amazement and then the smaller of the two cried out, 'Edleweiss? Edleweiss! Is it you? Oh my precious!' and she made a fantastic leap to land beside Blue's friend, who was still looking a little confused.

'Mama, is it you?' cried snow leopard. 'Mama, Mama, and Papa!' she purred with pure delight and the three of them pressed their heads against each other and tickled each other's faces with their fine whiskers.

'My lovely, *lovely* Edelweiss. I thought I would never see you again,' murmured the snow leopard's mother.

'Edelweiss!' called out Blue with a grin on her face. 'Our snow leopard is called Edelweiss,' she told everyone delightedly.

Chapter 17

Snow leopard, or rather Edelweiss, told her parents some of what had happened, but she also explained that there was no time to go into details. Twiggy needed help before she faded away completely.

'They talked about The Life Spirit,' prompted Blue, 'The Life Spirit seems to be the answer to our problems. Please ask who or what is The Life Spirit.'

'The Life Spirit is a spirit of the land who is all-powerful, but it is in the valley. How fast can you move?' asked Edelweiss's father.

Here Edelweiss shook her head sorrowfully and Blue listened to her explaining that the villagers did not move fast, the young were even slower and one was so ill that she had to be carried.

'It will take two days at least and, up here, there is a chance that we could set off the Great Avalanche,' explained Edelweiss's father. 'Everything below lives in fear as one day the avalanche will fall, but no one knows when. If it falls whilst we are on it,' he went on grimly, 'we will not live to tell the tale!'

'We need to find The Life Spirit. How *do* we get into the valley?' Jack demanded.

'All you have to do is call to him, and if you have a great need he will find you,' replied Edelweiss's mother.

'But come, I will show you the great obstacle,' and Edelweiss's father indicated that they should follow him.

They followed a rocky ledge round a corner. The father leopard transmitted more to Blue, who translated what he was saying, 'See that huge mound of snow? We will have to climb up above this snow field and hope that it does not avalanche and take us with it. We must make no noise and tread softly.'

They stared at the huge but seemingly innocent great bulge of snow just below them. It was like the softest pillow of swansdown, but deadly.

'If it avalanched today it would be good, as everything that is alive has been called to a Festival at the other end of the valley. But who can say when an avalanche is ready to fall. And if we set it off, how could we be sure that we would not fall with it? There it sits as a terrible menace to all of us.' The leopard shook his head and scraped his paw on the rock in frustration.

Jack edged past the others to look at the snow mass. His board was vibrating against his side. It was crying out to him, and Jack knew instinctively what he must do. There could be no discussion with the others, he knew they would stop him.

It was Theta who intuited what he was about to do.

To the father leopard's dismayed astonishment and incomprehension, Jack ran off the rocky ledge, holding his board in front of him., He landed with a mighty whump onto the great pillow of unstable snow.

There was a frenzied scream from Blue, 'Jack!' and a cry of 'No!' from Nick, mixed with horrified roars from the leopards.

For a long moment nothing happened. Then there was an ear-splitting BOOM which exploded from the snow mass and it started to move - slowly at first, then all of a sudden the great mass dropped off the mountainside. They watched as Jack fell with the avalanche and disappeared into a massive cloud of ice crystals.

Blue and Meesha threw their arms around each other and broke into terrible sobs. Nick sank to his knees. Tenzing stood with the three leopards, they all strained to see through the clouds of ice crystals that were billowing back up the mountain with such force, it took their breath away.

Tenzing shook his head. 'He has made the way safe, but at what cost?' he asked soberly. 'Because of his brave sacrifice, we must do our best to get Twiggy to somewhere she can get help.'

He went back to rally Blue and the sad little group. Although the wolves could scent that they were somewhere they could find food and make their home, they seemed loathe to leave Twiggy. They snuggled against her to keep her warm and made little whining noises in her ear.

Miserably they set off over the bare earth, all that was left now that the huge mass of snow had fallen off the side of the mountain. Around them icy particles that had blown back up the mountain side were settling. They could not bear to think that far below, caught up in the rocks and ice blocks was Jack's body. As they looked around, they could see that Theta was nowhere to be seen. Shocked, they realised that he too, must have been taken by the avalanche.

Chapter 18

Little did the sad group of travellers know that Jack was compelled by his snowboard to leap on to the snow mass. Jack knew he had to get to The Life Spirit as quickly as he could, but he did not know how urgently until his snowboard had insisted he jumped onto the unstable mass of snow.

As he felt the great weight of the blocks of ice shifting below him, a sense of excitement grew inside him. The snow shifted and he rose to his knees. It gathered speed, and he stood up on his board and rode on a great block of ice, that dropped through the vast space below. Together he and his board carved a route through the billowing snowflakes. Jack was gasping for breath, but nothing could stop the exhilaration of being part of the huge natural force of the avalanche.

Occasionally he was aware of horrified shrieks close to him making him wonder if there was not something else, like a bird, caught up in the avalanche too. Thousands of tons of rocks, ice blocks and snow hurtled to the valley and in seconds came to rest in a great tangled mass at the bottom. But on the top of the avalanche was Jack. Incredibly he landed as light as a feather on his board. He stepped off it and made a great cry of exultation towards the mountains.

'Oh my, oh my! I wanted to get home, and I knew it was only Avalanche Rider who could get me there, but I really thought the last part of the journey would be a bit less terrifying!' exclaimed a voice by his knees.

'Wow Theta! You came too?' asked Jack rather shocked to think he had been responsible for not only himself but Theta too.

'Didn't you feel me clinging on to you? What a terrible experience! I thought my last moments had arrived several times,' gasped Theta. 'But, oh, how wonderful to be back in my home valley. Oh look, its Wallace!'

Jack and Theta's arrival and Jack's cry of excitement had been witnessed by a curious creature hovering safely a little way off and covered with ice crystals. It looked like a huge beetle crossed with a bee.

It flew towards them.

'Well young man, you seem very pleased with yourself?' it spoke directly to Jack, and then, 'Welcome back Theta! Your family will be pleased to see you - but not so happy that you have brought humans into our valley. And look at this mess!' he buzzed.

Jack looked back at the tons of rock, ice, and snow. He could also see snapped trees and bits of wood that looked like parts of wooden cabins and furniture. He felt crestfallen. 'But I thought that the avalanche threatened the valley, and it was better to have it gone than hanging over you?' he explained in a small voice.

'Quite right too,' called out a cheerful voice and a figure, not unlike Theta arrived, carried by a little horse that picked its way over the debris, sometimes having to jump over the larger blocks of hardened snow.

'There certainly is lots of work to make good, but imagine what would have happened to the people who live in those houses if they had been in them. Instead, they are all partying in our yearly valley Festival. You have saved many families. I expect there will be a few grumbles. Can't be helped'.

Jack was feeling faint from the excitement of riding the avalanche, but he turned away from the irritable Wallace and towards the beautiful little horse and its imposing rider. It was with a trembling voice that he asked the rider where he could find The Life Spirit, 'My friend will die if she is not helped in some way very soon,' he wailed and looked at Theta to confirm his great need. But Theta was bowing to the horse and his rider.

'I AM The Life Spirit. I feel your need. And don't mind Wallace; he looks after unwanted visitors for me, but he is right: you and your friends MUST return from where you came.' He unstrapped a small pouch from his saddle. 'In this phial you will find a potion that will help your friend, but the question is how will we get it to her?'

Jack looked back at the devastation now blocking the lower part of the mountain. To his despair he realised that getting back to Twiggy would take days. He sat down hard, feeling the last of his strength ebbing out of him.

But as he experienced a sense of defeat, he saw Theta put his hands to his lips and call loudly into the sky. Almost at once there was a bugling cry, followed by another cry; it came from lower down the valley. Shortly after, they could all see three V shapes coming towards them in the sky and as they came closer Jack realised it was the demoiselle cranes! They landed beside

Jack and smacked their long bills and danced on their spindly legs round him. He recognised the mother and her son who were on the ledge on the other side of the mountain range. It was the weak son that Twiggy had given the bee sweet to, but now he looked strong and eager! Theta talked to them in his strange language.

'The cranes will take you back up the mountain,' he announced proudly.

'Please there is no time to lose!' gasped Jack.

'Not so fast,' interrupted The Life Spirit. 'When you find your friends, you *must* return to your human life. There is no place for you in this valley. Just the four of you must go; no one else. You must go back to The Fault and follow the white lights.'

'Yes, yes,' agreed Jack, eager now to get back to Twiggy.

And before he could thank The Life Spirit, it had disappeared.

The male demoiselle crane crouched low in front of him so he could clamber onto its back, the precious phial in his hand.

'Oh Theta, I won't see you again?' called Jack sadly to Theta.

'Who knows Jack, who knows where Avalanche Rider will take you? Perhaps our paths *will* cross again. Good luck my friend. Thank you for releasing me from the attic!'

The cranes ran along the ground and then all three soared into the air.

They circled their way up the mountain, using the up draughts to carry them. Jack was riding the biggest, he assumed this was the father. The female took his snowboard, and the youngest flew beside them, bugling a cheerful call, and searching for the rest of their party, and most importantly Twiggy.

Not far from the mouth of the cave, they spotted the forlorn group, and alighted beside them. The birds eyed the wolves and leopards warily.

Everyone called out Jack's name with such delighted surprise, that for a moment he felt overcome and could not move or see, as tears filled his eyes.

Then he ran towards Twiggy holding out the phial. Meesha poured its contents into Twiggy's mouth and watched anxiously. Nothing happened. Then Meesha felt her pulse and looked up nodding.

'It's stronger,' she confirmed.

'Then we must go back to the cave, we have to get back to our world, please help us carry Twiggy?' Everyone was now in awe of Jack so, without further question, Tenzing lifted Twiggy, and they all went back to the cave.

Into the warm air they walked until they were at the lip of the chasm. This time Tenzing and Meesha nodded without comment as Jack told them they could not come too.

'For many years we have been dreaming of a new land. We are ready for a new challenge,' they reassured him. They all hugged each other. Blue hugged Edelweiss especially hard. Jack's board thrummed, Blue grabbed Jack, and Nick held up Twiggy who could now stand, but she still looked terribly weak. Tenzing handed them their ski boots.

Jack bowed to the wolves, and then to Meesha and Tenzing. 'It's not enough to say thank you, but that is all I can do: thank you,' he said.

'Ready?' he asked Blue and Nick, they nodded. And all of them, led by Jack and his board, leapt into the abyss. Behind them they heard the wolves howling and Edelweiss and her parents roaring.

'Goodbye, dear Edelweiss,' cried out Blue, and now Twiggy mustered up enough energy to call goodbye to the wolves.

Jack had to drive his board down towards the white lights. Sometimes a sparkling green light would catch his attention and his board would hesitate as if to wait for another command. But although Jack was tempted to following the sparkling green lights, he forced himself to refocus on the white lights.

On they went into a dream world until they were rudely awoken by the shock of cold. Men in uniform were hovering over them. And the huge noise of a helicopter landing next to them brought them into their world with a rude jolt.

Chapter 19

'Your name, your name?' asked a man, who was clearly a medic, to Jack. Jack could hear Blue and Nick being asked the same questions. He could hear Blue insisting she was fine.

He saw a figure on a stretcher being placed into the helicopter. It lifted away and disappeared, blowing snow all over them with a loud clatter of blades.

'How is Twiggy?' he asked the medic who was wrapping him in foil and now picking him up to put him on a sledge. 'I can walk,' he protested. But he was pressed down and zipped up.

'Don't forget my board!' he cried out as the sledge started to move down the slope.

He was aware that Blue and Nick were in sledges beside him, and as they were taken down the mountain, he realised that he was incredibly tired. He was taken to a Medical Centre and placed in a room with Blue. A few minutes later not only their father appeared, but their mother too.

'How long have we been missing?' asked Blue.

'Thirty-six hours,' replied their father, 'and we have been desperately worried every second of them,' he added.

Their mother could hardly talk, she hugged both of them and cried.

After a few tests, the doctors announced that incredibly Blue, Jack and Nick had suffered no ill effects and could go back to their hotel. They also said that Twiggy was very dehydrated but since she had been put on a drip, she was responding well and would probably be released in 24 hours.

Everyone asked how they had survived so well. To this there was no answer. Apparently, Twiggy had talked about another world, with wolves and snow leopards, but this talk was dismissed as delusions brought on by her brain starved of liquid.

After hearing that, Jack and Blue found it easier to say that they didn't remember anything at all, except being hungry, thirsty, and cold. Nick was in another room, so they had no idea what he was saying.

'He always believed the whole thing was a sort of nightmare anyway,' pointed out Blue when they chatted privately together.

It was decided they would finish their holiday. Aunt Tatine had agreed to have their mother to stay for free and their mother's partner. Jack did not know that her mother had a partner, but when he met Harry, as he was called, he seemed nice.

They all shared an early supper together.

'Worrying about us all has made Mum and Dad friends again,' Blue said quietly to Jack. He nodded happily.

In the middle of supper Nick and his mother passed them. To everyone's amazement Nick stopped to announce, 'You are a real hero Jack!'

Jack blushed, feeling incredibly embarrassed.

But Blue agreed; 'We wouldn't be here if it wasn't for Jack!'

Nick's mother patted Jack on his back in the way that a person does, if they haven't the slightest idea of what their son is talking about but feels that some sort of applauding action is called for.

And next, their ski instructors called into the hotel to see the missing 'Braves,' as they called them.

'There 'eez the visitors races tomorrow, what a pity you cannot compete,' said his instructor mournfully.

'Why can't I?' asked Jack.

'Oh! darling you won't be strong enough. You need a day's rest at least,' insisted his mother.

'I feel completely fine. Mum, I will be devastated if I can't race!' said Jack with horror all over his face.

'Henry?' His mother turned to his father for support.

'Well, the medics said that they could find nothing wrong with them, and I have just had a text to say that Twiggy has responded so well to treatment that she will be released later on this evening.'

'Henry you are such a push over. What do you think Marine?' appealed his mother.

'If 'ee promises to stop the moment 'ee doz not feel 'imself, perhaps 'ee can go. - 'ee 'as a natural ability,' she reassured Jack's mother.

'Outvoted Mum,' stated Blue, but she hugged her mother to soften the blow.

'Let's see how you all feel tomorrow. We can decide then,' suggested Harry. This sensible suggestion suited everybody.

To everyone's delight a wan Twiggy returned to the hotel. Blue was not allowed to share a room with her, to make sure she had a full night's sleep. But they had a quick conversation on their room telephones.

'Everyone says, I am suffering from delirium, when I tell them what happened,' Twiggy complained. 'What did they say to you?'

Blue had to admit that they had not dared tell anyone what they had been through ... it was too fantastical.

'But it did happen!' insisted Twiggy. 'Didn't it?'

'Of course it did, but think about it Twiggy, how could we tell them about a snow leopard called Edelweiss who could talk to me?' There was a small silence on the other end of the phone.

'I don't remember a snow leopard, but I *do* remember wolves,' said Twiggy.

'Wolves?' questioned Blue, disbelievingly. Jack gesticulated wildly, 'Tell her I remember Edelweiss!' he hissed. 'And the wolves!' he added.

To his horror further questioning showed that both girls only remembered bits of their adventure. The conversation was stopped abruptly when Twiggy's mother insisted Twiggy went straight to sleep. And it was not long before Blue and Jack's parents were insisting the same thing.

'We shall talk about it tomorrow with Nick,' promised Blue. But she could hear that Jack was fast asleep. One arm hung over the edge of the bed and she could see the red marks on his wrists where he had clung onto the board.

'Explain how these bruises happened,' she challenged imaginary medics.

The next day, they found that everyone in the hotel knew that they had been missing, and lots of people wanted to shake their hands or ruffle their hair and announce how happy they were to see them safe.

Blue could not help giggling when she saw Nick ducking, as a guest meaning well, tried to give him a hug.

The three families greeted each other over breakfast.

'Now, are you sure you want to do the races?' asked Jack's father.

'I want to,' said Jack firmly.

'Me too,' added Blue.

'How's your father?' asked Blue kindly.

'He's fine,' answered Nick's mother, 'but we are catching a plane tonight to be with him.'

'I am going to watch you race and cheer you on; we have time before we fly home,' announced Nick, much to the surprise of Henry and Marine.

'Good 'eavens, 'e really 'as changed 'is tune?' said Marine to Jack as Nick and his mother went to their table.

'He's OK,' nodded Blue.

'Jack?' questioned Marine.

'Yes,' agreed Jack 'I think I can say he is a friend now!' he said surprising Marine.

At that moment his mother joined them with Harry and gave Blue and Jack a crushing hug.

'Your Aunt Tatine has been such a kind hostess,' she told Marine.

Pierre arrived with extra cups, and they all sat round the table drinking coffee and chatting.

'Are you racing Pierre?' asked Henry.

'I am,' he replied, 'I shall be in a different class, but I will be cheering Jack and Blue.'

'And we shall cheer *you* on,' said Blue, blushing.

Everything seemed perfect, until Jack discovered that his board was nowhere to be found. He was so dismayed, that his father felt compelled to ring the Security to find out if they had found his board but forgotten to bring it to him. There was no board to be found.

'But I had it, just before we were put on the sledges!' he wailed. Further enquiries were hopeless; no one could remember him having a board. Jack felt completely bereft.

Connor from the ski hire said that as it had snowed all night they would not be able to find the board, or the others' skiis, until the snow thawed again.

'When will that be?' asked Jack miserably.

'Likely spring,' replied Connor, grimacing when he saw the horror on Jack's face. 'Look man, I shall ski down there sometimes and keep a look out, OK?'

Jack nodded unhappily.

'Hey, I have a really nice board here. You can have it for the afternoon, don't have to pay a thing!' stated Connor kindly.

Jack mumbled his thanks. *But there is only one board for me,* he thought sadly to himself.

Later, he couldn't help but brighten up as they approached the area where the races were taking place. A powerful beat was coming from two huge speakers. Every so often the music would stop and an announcer would explain what was going on. All along the race track there were spectators, many of them carrying a cup of hot wine and the smell of cloves and cinnamon seasoned the air.

Marine and his mother had chosen to wait at the bottom of the run. Blue, Jack and his father took a lift to the top.

Amongst the racers waiting to go was Pierre.

'Good luck Pierre!' shouted Blue. He waved back and came over to talk.

'I go in about ten minutes,' he told them. 'Be careful Jack. Gates 5 and 6, they are vairy near to the ozzer one; it 'ees necessary to prepare for 6, almost before you are passed 5. OK?'

Jack suddenly felt excited, 'Ok Pierre!'

Ten minutes passed in a flash, and it was Pierre's turn to go. He slipped through the gate and they watched him flashing down the run, and then disappearing round a corner.

'He looked pretty fast,' commented Henry approvingly. It was not long before they saw Pierre again as when he got to the bottom, he caught the lift up again, to come and help get Blue and Jack started.

The racers were thinning out: they had started with the older and more experienced skiers, and now only younger people were left. Blue's class started.

'Good luck Blue,' they cried as she pushed off taking the first turn neatly.

At last it was Jack's turn, it had all become a little slower and lots of people in his class had fallen. Jack had hardly had a practise on the new board. But as he started down the slope, the sensation of riding the avalanche came back to him. He picked up speed and felt the thrill of slipping headlong down the racetrack. He counted the gates and braked slightly so he could flash through numbers 5 and wow, 6 *did* come up quickly, but he was through safely, and it seemed in no time he was hurtling through the finishing line.

For the onlookers it was particularly exciting as the commentator told them that Jack was not only fast for his class, but he had in fact gone faster than most of the classes above him. Everyone hugged and kissed him, including Twiggy, who told him he was 'brilliant', which made him feel especially warm inside.

Prize giving was back at the hotel. It seemed that news of Jack's prowess had gone before him, because before they announced the winners and gave them their medals, a man approached Jack's parents. He said that he represented a company that sponsored gifted athletes and they would like to consider a scholarship for Jack, to return next winter and train to become a racing snowboarder.

'Would you like that Jack?' asked his father, rather overwhelmed by this offer.

'You could stay with Aunt Tatine I am sure,' offered Marine.

'Like it? I'd really love it Dad!' exclaimed Jack.

Later on, when they were sitting in the hotel lounge, Nick joined them. They told him what had happened.

'That would be good, you might be able to find your board Jack, and you might be able to find the entrance to the cave again, and show all these people who don't believe what happened to us.'

'I miss Edelweiss,' said Blue a little forlornly. 'But Nick you believed it was all a dream yourself!' she accused him.

'That horrible woman who whacked me over my nose, that wasn't a dream. They x-rayed it and I have a cracked nose and it still hurts if I touch it!'

They became silent for a moment, as each one tried to recapture the memories of the last few days.

'Hey you guys, the disco has started, come on Blue, I want to show you some sexy moves!' laughed Pierre. They all got up and joined him. They danced in a group.

'I don't care whether we are believed or not,' said Jack to himself. 'This has been a brilliant holiday. Next year, perhaps I will be able to come back and train, with a scholarship.' The moment he thought that, the music changed to a peculiar thrumming.

'Hey, Jack, it sounds like Avalanche Rider!' shouted Twiggy.

Jack could feel a vibration inside of him. He was sure it *was* Avalanche Rider trying to communicate with him.

He felt sad they were flying first thing the next day, but he made a promise to himself. He *would* come back and perhaps he would reconnect with Theta. But above all he *would* find his beautiful board Avalanche Rider, and ride it again…

The End

With thanks to the following who made suggestions and corrections:

Hermione, Charlotte Cavaghan, my husband David.

Above all I am hugely grateful to my eldest son James, who believed in the venture by reading the book to his children, illustrating the front page and publishing it onto Amazon.

Printed in Great Britain
by Amazon